# ROGUE

A NOVEL BY

## LYN MILLER-LACHMANN

NANCY PAULSEN BOOKS

AN IMPRINT OF PENGUIN GROUP (USA) INC.

NANCY PAULSEN BOOKS • An imprint of Penguin Young Readers Group.

Published by The Penguin Group.

Penguin Group (USA) Inc., 375 Hudson Street, New York, NY 10014, USA.

Penguin Group (Canada), 90 Eglinton Avenue East, Suite 700, Toronto,
Ontario M4P 2Y3, Canada (a division of Pearson Penguin Canada Inc.).

Penguin Books Ltd, 80 Strand, London WC2R 0RL, England.

Penguin Ireland, 25 St. Stephen's Green, Dublin 2, Ireland (a division of Penguin Books Ltd).

Penguin Group (Australia), 707 Collins Street, Melbourne, Victoria 3008, Australia
(a division of Pearson Australia Group Pty Ltd).

Penguin Books India Pvt Ltd, 11 Community Centre,
Panchsheel Park, New Delhi—110 017, India.

Penguin Group (NZ), 67 Apollo Drive, Rosedale, Auckland 0632, New Zealand
(a division of Pearson New Zealand Ltd).

Penguin Books South Africa, Rosebank Office Park, 181 Jan Smuts Avenue,
Parktown North 2193, South Africa.

Penguin China, B7 Jiaming Center, 27 East Third Ring Road North,
Chaoyang District, Beijing 100020, China.

Penguin Books Ltd, Registered Offices: 80 Strand, London WC2R 0RL, England.

Published simultaneously in Canada. Printed in the United States of America.

Design by Marikka Tamura.

Text set in New Century Schoolbook.

Library of Congress Cataloging-in-Publication Data
Miller-Lachmann, Lyn, 1956–
Rogue / Lyn Miller-Lachmann.   pages cm
Summary: An eighth-grade girl with Asperger's syndrome tries to befriend
her new neighbor, facing many challenges along the way.
[1. Asperger's syndrome—Fiction. 2. Autism—Fiction. 3. Interpersonal relations—Fiction.
4. Friendship—Fiction. 5. Racially mixed people—Fiction.] I. Title.
PZ7.M6392Ro 2013   [Fic]—dc23   2012036570
ISBN 978-0-399-16225-1
1 3 5 7 9 10 8 6 4 2

*To my Secret Gardeners*

## CHAPTER 1

*IT USUALLY TOOK THE NEW KIDS TWO WEEKS TO DUMP ME,* three weeks at the most. Melanie Prince-Parker was the quickest. She moved from West Hartford to Willingham when we started eighth grade. I couldn't make her sit across from me for more than five minutes of lunch, and at the end of the first week I spotted her in the middle of the popular girls' table.

I wanted to know how she did it.

I wanted to *be* Melanie Prince-Parker.

I used to watch her at lunchtime, first sitting at a table on the same side of the cafeteria, then moving closer and closer until one March day I set my tray at a corner of the table where the popular girls always sat.

The girls instantly stopped talking. Melanie scraped her chair back and stood. I lowered my gaze but could feel her glare on my face.

Without a word, Melanie pushed my tray from the table.

I jumped backward. The clatter of plastic on tile broke

*1*

the silence. The tip of the apple pie stuck out from an edge of overturned plate. Oily tomato sauce spread from a pile of sloppy joe toward the bun that rolled away. Wilted lettuce curled up next to the pale green tray.

Kids surrounded me, shouting. Voices rose from the chorus.

*Ooh, snap!*

*What was she thinking?*

*You don't do that, sit anywhere you want.*

*That's retarded.*

*So weird.*

*Look, she's crying again. Crybaby Kiara!*

*Crybaby Kiara!*

Through blurry eyes, I stared at my trembling hands. A clear droplet splashed on my wrist, but I hadn't heard myself crying with all the noise, the kids laughing.

Anger surged from the pit of my empty stomach. My ears burned. I had a right to sit where I wanted. This wasn't kindergarten where they assigned seats in the lunchroom.

I picked up the tray.

For a moment, I caught Melanie's eyes. Scary eyes. Deep brown irises. My mind flashed to my mother's eyes, what they looked like whenever I made Mami mad. Melanie wore black eyeliner like Mami too.

I hadn't seen those eyes since Mami left last month.

I raised the tray above me, a batter waiting for the pitch.

Melanie placed her hands on her hips and opened her mouth. Her soprano harmonized with the chorus around me.

"Don't be stupid, Kiara. Put the tray down."

I swung.

I swung at the light brown face that contained those evil eyes. The tray slammed into her face. Shock waves vibrated in my arms and spread to the rest of my body. I let go of the tray. It bounced on my foot before hitting the tile with a thud.

Laughter turned to screams. Melanie's nose spurted blood. Past her lips, down her chin, onto her pink sweater.

Then somebody's huge arms locked around me and carried me away.

Away from the cafeteria—and out of that school.

# CHAPTER 2

*CHAD ELLIOTT IS THE NEWEST NEW KID, THE NINTH SINCE* I started keeping track in third grade. Every year I'd go up to them and introduce myself—*Hi, I'm Kiara Thornton-Delgado. What's your name?* I said it to Chad two days ago when they moved in, but his father ordered him to carry boxes and not waste time on chitchat.

"I follow a band around the country," I tell Chad now. So he'll think I'm cool and like me. We're standing in the little park behind my house and across the street from his new home on the first floor of the Mackenzies' house.

He flashes me a snaggle-toothed smile, holds up two fingers in a peace sign, and says, "Woo, hoo. Grateful Dead, man."

The way he says it, I don't think he's impressed. Like I said something stupid—again.

I turn my face away and stare at the wooden fence that separates the park from my backyard. The late-afternoon sun casts shadows of Chad and me, making us look like stretched-out black-and-white drawings on the fence. Like a frame in a comic book.

"My parents are *in* the band. So are my brothers. And my uncles," I tell Chad. It's not quite the truth. But it *was*.

Chad hops onto the concrete platform that once was a stage and spins like a Tilt-A-Whirl, arms outstretched and blond hair flying. Above him, a squirrel darts across a bare branch. Mid-April in the northeastern corner of Connecticut means the buds still haven't opened on our late-blooming trees. "What's the band called?" he asks.

"Corazón del Este. 'Heart of the East' in Spanish."

"Never heard of 'em." He jumps down to the cobblestone path that runs from the platform like the center aisle of a theater. His feet slide on soggy leaves.

"They play folk music from around the world. They've played with Pete Seeger."

"Who's that?"

"You don't know?" Chad has to know. Pete Seeger is my family's hero. I've heard his name since I was old enough to understand words.

"Sounds like a loser band."

"No, they're not." I blink rapidly against the tears filling my eyes, tears for the band that hadn't made music together in nearly a year.

"Why're you crying?"

"I'm *not* crying." I wipe my eyes with my shirtsleeve so New Kid won't know me as Crybaby Kiara on the first day we've really met.

5

Chad turns his back on me and gazes across quiet Cherry Street to the sagging two-story house where his family now lives. The bottom floor used to be a second-hand record and comic book store, where I'd go after school to help Mr. Mackenzie shelve the stock and ring up sales until he died last year. Mr. Mac introduced me to the X-Men. The X-Men are mutants who don't fit into society. They're like me, but all of them have special powers. I'm still trying to find mine.

I blink hard, pretending to have dirt in my eye. Behind Chad two squirrels chase each other across the grass and spiral up the trunk of an oak tree. The one in the lead twitches its tail, as if to say *bet you can't catch me* to its friend. "My dad got this park built," I finally say.

"Huh?" Chad steps closer. He's a few inches shorter than me and skinny, with a narrow face, smooth cheeks, and a pointy nose. He looks more like a ten-year-old than a seventh-grader. His breath smells of minty gum.

I inch backward. "Here. Where we are."

Chad points to the brand-new wooden sign on the corner closest to Cherry Street and busy Washington Avenue. "Is your dad named—?"

"Nigel Mackenzie? No."

"Mackenzie? Isn't that the name of the lady whose boxes are upstairs—"

"He and Dad worked together to turn some empty lots into a park."

They'd originally planned to name the park after Dad, because when he first got cancer, the doctors didn't think they could cure him. When Dad did get cured, and the park finally got built, it was just called Cherry Street Park because Dad said he and Mr. Mac didn't like the idea of naming places after people who were still alive.

Now the park has Mr. Mac's name. It seems the whole town of Willingham wanted to remember Mr. Mac, and I don't understand why Mrs. Mac shut down the store and moved to her sister's house two towns away, as if she wanted to erase every trace of him. Dad said she didn't want to keep living in the place where her husband died, but I don't believe ghosts haunt those places and I don't see how moving away can make someone forget.

Mami moved away and I haven't forgotten her.

"How come you weren't on the bus?" Chad says, still staring at his house as if expecting something scary like Mr. Mac's ghost to burst out of it. Someone has covered the inside of the basement windows with what looks like black construction paper.

"I don't go to school anymore."

"You have to go to school."

"I'm homeschooled."

Chad whirls around so fast that strands of hair stick to his lips. "Hey, wait. Aren't you"—he snaps his fingers—"the psycho eighth-grader that got kicked out for throwing a lunch tray and busting someone's nose?"

"That's someone else. I, uh, travel with the band." Truth is, I didn't *throw* the tray. I slammed it—hands still on the tray. "Do you like the house?" I ask to change the subject.

"It's cool. I got my own room." He jumps up and down as

if trying to keep warm. "Last place I had to share with my little brother. He talks in his sleep."

"Is it the room by the kitchen or the one next to the front room?"

"How come you know the rooms?"

"I used to work there, when it was a music store." I sweep my hand in a semicircle to keep hyper Chad from running into me. "The store used to have concerts in this park too. Every Friday in the summer. Folk music. Hip-hop . . ."

"Hip-hop?" Chad's voice rises to a squeak.

"Yeah. Kids from the high school performed."

Chad stops jumping. "Cool!"

"But not anymore. Mr. Mackenzie, who owned the store, died last August." I gaze at the cobblestones, then at the house's second floor. "Heart attack. Upstairs. That's why they named the park after him."

Chad makes a shivery sound. I bet he does believe in ghosts.

And while I want him to like me, I don't like that he's living there.

The squeal of tires interrupts us. I spin around to face the corner, in time to see a gray car cut off traffic to make a wide left turn from busy Washington Avenue onto Cherry Street. Brakes screech and a horn blares. The car's tires bump the curb and . . . SMASH!

The crash on impact is followed by a longer crunch. Chad screams behind me. In the driveway, Mrs. Mac's gray Honda Civic has slammed the back of the Elliotts' rusted blue minivan.

Chad and I dash across the street.

Mrs. Mac's car smells like burnt plastic. Steam rises from the creased hood as her car's life hisses away. The deflated airbag hangs over the steering wheel. Slowly, the door opens. A leg pokes out—mostly covered by a paisley-print skirt and boots.

"Are you okay?" I ask Mrs. Mac.

Swearing, Chad runs his hand along his family's dented van and peers underneath.

Holding the door frame, Mrs. Mac pushes herself out of the car. Strands of her long charcoal-gray hair have come out of her braid. I know I should take her arm and help her, but I step back instead.

"I'm all right, don't call the cops." She sounds like she's speaking from far away. "One more accident and they'll yank my license." She flashes me a weak smile.

Mr. Mac used to do all their driving. He said she gave him a heart attack every time she got behind the wheel. But he didn't die in a car. He died in his bed.

She totters up the porch steps, fumbles with her keys to the door that leads upstairs, and drops them at her feet. They bounce off one black boot tip and slip through a gap in the floorboards. She grabs the doorknob. "Oh. They fell."

"Do you want me . . . to . . . look for them?" I ask, trembling inside. Once a cat died under the Mackenzies' porch. Its bones are probably still there.

"Please, dear." In her tiny, distant voice, she adds, "I'm sorry. I don't know what's gotten into me."

Chad stands behind me, his face pale. He shoves his hands into the kangaroo pockets of his navy New England Patriots hoodie, making no move to rescue me.

I crouch down and reach blindly under the porch steps for Mrs. Mac's keys. My fingertips touch only air, a spiderweb, a dead insect in the web. I force myself to look. In the dim light I see the keys lying in the dirt and next to them a white plastic bottle with a skull and crossbones and the word POISON stamped in black on the label. Swallowing to keep my stomach in place, I read the words *Muriatic Acid* and below, *Ácido Muriático,* the name of the mysterious acid in Spanish. Avoiding the bottle, I close my fingers around the keys and pull them out. I take them up to her on the porch, where she squeezes my shoulder. I swallow again because strangers touching me creeps me out and even though I've known Mrs. Mac my entire life, today she feels like a stranger.

"Did you hit your head, Mrs. Mac?" I glance down at Chad, who has taken my spot on the first porch step. "He can call the ambulance."

"No," Chad whispers.

"No ambulance, no police," Mrs. Mac says. "Your parents, Charles. Are they home?"

"It's Chad. And they ain't home." His voice is hard and his hands still in his pockets.

"Tell them I'll make good. Send me the bill, and I'll deduct it from the rent." She scrapes the key into the lock and opens the door. I notice a stack of boxes at the top of the stairs and wonder how long it will take for her to have all the rooms totally empty—nothing left of the times she and Mr. Mac took care of me like grandparents while the rest of my family went on tour. "Thank you, dear Kiara." Before going inside, she kisses my forehead. I cringe and rub my forehead with the back of my hand while the door closes behind her. I didn't expect her to kiss me. I hadn't seen her in nearly a month.

"She's drunk." Chad pounds his fist into the palm of his hand.

"No, she isn't. Her husband died. She barely knows how to drive." My shoulder and forehead still feel crawly. I remember the times I leaned against her while she read to me and kissed me on the top of my head. She smelled of the wild honeysuckle in her garden then.

Chad points at the two cars, navy and gray, crumpled together. "My parents are gonna kill me."

"Why? It wasn't your fault."

"I'm here. That's enough. Anyway, you heard her. No cops."

"Yeah." I see my chance with New Kid. Keep him from getting in trouble with his parents. "Want to come over?"

Chad's eyes dart up and down the street. "Can't. I have to stay here till they tell me. Till they . . . get back." I wonder what the van's doing there if his parents aren't home. Then again, no one came outside when Mrs. Mac rammed it.

"I'll wait with you. Tell them what happened." I don't want to leave him alone to get in trouble. No—I don't want to leave him to maybe find another friend and ditch me like the other eight New Kids did. But seeing him twitch and fidget and glance from corner to corner like he's watching three Ping-Pong games at once is making me fidgety too. And the wind is picking up, shifting to the north, blowing colder from the tops of the tall trees as dusk creeps in.

"No. Just go," he says.

I do what he tells me. Because it's what all the kids tell me, and I haven't figured out how to make them change their minds.

## CHAPTER 3

*I CROSS NIGEL MACKENZIE PARK AND SQUEEZE THROUGH A* gap in the fence to my backyard. The high fence and setting sun cast shadows across the grass. I sniff the honeysuckle bushes Mami transplanted from the Mackenzies' years ago. A tire swing hangs from a branch of our giant oak tree. Underneath it, the grass is scuffed to bare dirt. Here's where I pretend to be my favorite X-Men character, Rogue. In my mind, the oak tree becomes a cypress tree and the tire swing is a rope hanging over a bayou. I climb onto the tire, swing a few times, then jump off and land in a defensive crouch. I hold out my arms, one at a time, throwing imaginary fireballs. Then I practice a few karate kicks and end up on my butt.

*A Hyper Chad move,* I think. I hope he doesn't get into trouble for the accident Mrs. Mac caused.

Dad must have left the back door unlocked when he got home from work, and when it closes, it skims my heel.

Guitar chords in minor keys rise from the small room off the kitchen, which used to be a pantry until he turned it into a recording studio. The door is open, but judging from the slow, mournful melody, I don't think he wants to talk.

A box of spaghetti sits on the counter next to a jar of tomato sauce. The same dinner three nights in a row.

Dad's random chords segue into the Jackson Browne song "How Long." The band used to play that song all the time. It was one of the dozen or so that Mami sang in English, and she sang it so beautifully that half the people in the audience wiped their eyes with tissues. When Dad plays the melody, I know he misses Mami. It also means I'll be cooking dinner tonight because he's too depressed to do it himself.

I pour myself a glass of milk and put a pot of water on the stove to boil. I have ten minutes until I have to add the spaghetti, so I go upstairs to my room, flop onto my bed, and stare at the poster on the ceiling. "Hey, Rogue," I say out loud. "I think I found a friend. His name is Chad."

Rogue stares back at me. Actually, Anna Paquin playing Rogue stares at me, and I wish they'd gotten me to play her instead. She's just an actress and I'm the real thing.

Rogue's wavy hair matches my hair. Mine falls to the middle of my back. It's cut in layers, a perfect combination of Mami's dark brown hair and Dad's light brown hair that goes to honey blond in the summer. I comb it over my right eye just like Rogue does, and one of these days I'm going to get that blond streak in front too. Like Rogue I don't wear makeup, because it takes too much time to put on and gets in the way when you're trying to be a superhero. In the poster on my ceiling, Rogue is dressed in black leather and looks away, down at her feet and a little to the left. She looks at the same spot I do when I talk to people.

Rogue's real name is Anna Marie. She's Cajun, from the bayous of Mississippi. Her parents were hippies like Dad—who met Mami at a music festival and dropped out of college after Mami got pregnant with my oldest brother, Eli. And when Anna Marie was fourteen, her mother left her family, just like my mother left me. Once I became obsessed with Rogue, I read everything I could about Cajuns and decorated my walls with pictures of bayous and cypress trees, cooking posters with recipes for gumbo and jambalaya, and maps. Because of her, I decided to take French last year. Mami, who fled the war in El Salvador with her mother and brothers when she was a teenager, wanted me to sign up for Spanish.

"Why should I take Spanish with beginners when I've spoken it all my life?" I asked.

"Because you don't know how to read and write it. And I don't have time to teach you." Her father had taught high school before he died in the war, so reading and writing are important to her.

And already *je parle français mieux que les étudiants en l'ecole secondaire,* mainly from websites and the free videos I've downloaded. Now that I'm not in school, I have to teach myself French, and I'm learning a lot faster than I did in a class where the students acted up and took forever to figure things out. Ms. Latimer, the homeschool teacher the district sent me, comes two hours a day to cover English, math, science, and social studies, and the rest of the time, I get turned loose to study with Mr. Internet.

I'm typing *muriatic acid* into Google when I hear voices below.

I make out Dad's. And Mrs. Mac's. I check the clock at the bottom of my computer screen.

Six thirty-five. I forgot the water on the stove. And my promise to be extra helpful ever since I got kicked out of school.

I scramble downstairs, expecting to smell scorched pot the closer I get to the kitchen. Conversation stops me before I turn the corner from the living room. No burning odor. Someone—Dad or Mrs. Mac—must have taken care of the water for me. I press myself against the wall to listen.

"Are you still homeschooling her?" Mrs. Mac doesn't sound nearly as shaky as she did after the accident.

"Don't have a choice, Dee."

"You should get her counseling too. It's helped me after Nigel . . ."

I'm not so sure about that. Mrs. Mac did wreck two cars today. But Dad doesn't say what I'm thinking. In fact, he doesn't say anything.

"It's not right to let her struggle."

I turn Mrs. Mac's words over in my mind. Is that what I'm doing? *Struggling?*

I hold my breath, waiting for Dad to say what I think he's going to say. What he says to Ms. Latimer. That I'm immature. That I can't control my anger—or my tears. That I miss my mother.

"What do you think I should do?" Dad finally asks.

"You can get her a diagnosis. Nigel and I wondered if she might have something else. Something related to autism."

"So they can put her in special-needs classes rather than the honors classes where she belongs? If Yasmín found out they weren't letting her reach her potential . . ."

"She's not here, J.T. You have to do what's right for Kiara."

"Which is getting her back to school." After a few seconds of silence, he says, "God, I wish Yasmín was here . . ."

"It's tough being alone. I know. But you can get help."

"Kiara doesn't need a shrink."

The clattering of pots ends the discussion, but it doesn't stop my mind from stirring their words and a lot of other scary stuff too. When Ms. Latimer told Dad they might put me in a special-needs class in high school next year, I asked Mr. Internet about "special-needs kids" and at the top of a list called Alphabet Soup found Asperger's syndrome.

I wonder if that's what Rogue has, why she can't touch people or be touched and why she has to absorb their emotions, which she does when she touches someone. Her emotions didn't develop the way they were supposed to because of a mutation.

I can't tell Dad or Mrs. Mac what Eli said to Max when they came home from their college spring break last month—the week before I got kicked out of school—but I can't forget it either. Sometimes the words knock around the inside of my skull so fast I'm afraid they're going to burst out without me saying them.

I shouldn't have stood in the hall while they talked about Mami that morning—just like I shouldn't be eavesdropping now. Back when my brothers lived at home, I used to listen outside their shared bedroom all the time, trying to discover the secrets of making friends and what it was like to have them.

"I heard her sing in Montreal last week," Max said. Because he goes to the University of Vermont, he's close enough to visit her. And he's always been the one most into music—like her. "She sounds better than ever. And she's happy to be performing again."

"Glad someone's happy," Eli said. "And it pays a lot more than tutoring or cleaning houses while Corazón del Este fell apart bit by bit."

Eli was right about the bit-by-bit part. Three years ago he won a scholarship for a premed program at Boston College. After he left home, the band started getting fewer gigs. Dad got a job at Tech Town and Mami as a house cleaner, which made it even harder for them to travel to their remaining gigs. Then my two uncles returned to Montreal, where their mother, my *abuela,* lived. And when Max started college last fall, the band broke up for good.

"Eli, this is a once-in-a-lifetime opportunity. To be a backup vocalist for one of Canada's greatest singers. She's going to take Mami to the next level for sure." Max p

"And, get this."

"What, bro?"

"I'm going to audition for her band soon as school's out."

"Good for you, Max. Good for Mami. Totally stinks for Kiara, though." I held my breath at Eli's mention of my name. "I mean, we're in college, so it doesn't matter as much. But imagine living with someone as helpless as Dad. Then imagine that person being Kiara."

A cry caught in my throat. At least Dad had stuck around to take care of me. Mami hadn't.

"Poor Kiara," Max said. "There's no way he can handle her."

Then Eli lowered his voice, as if he had the special power to see me through walls. "There's something I found out in my molecular biology course this semester. The chemotherapy they gave Dad way back when he had cancer. It causes genetic mutations. That's probably why Kiara is—"

"Different," Max finished.

*A mutant. Like Rogue. Contaminated with toxic chemicals.*

"Well, I hope Dad gets it together to get her some help," Eli said. "Because Mami was good with her. She got Kiara to talk to people like a normal person instead of staring at the floor or throwing a tantrum for no reason."

I didn't understand. How could Mami be so good with me if she left me?

## CHAPTER 4

*I PUSH MY HEAD AGAINST THE WALL THAT HIDES ME FROM* my father and Mrs. Mac. No more listening to other people talk about me when they think I can't hear them. I have to make them understand.

After a deep breath, I step into the kitchen. "I know what's wrong with me."

Dad looks up from the pan of spaghetti sauce. He hasn't taken off his blue vest from his job at the Tech Town in Manchester. His name tag reads JEREMY T. as if he's a kid in elementary school, not the guitarist J. T. Thornton of Corazón del Este. Mrs. Mac holds the oven mitts. Cloudy water gushes over the top of the spaghetti pot and sizzles when it hits the stove.

I try to meet their eyes but end up watching the boiling water retreat to the inside of the pot as soon as Mrs. Mac turns off the gas. "It *is* a type of autism. Asperger's syndrome," I say.

"That's what I tried to tell you, J.T." Mrs. Mac slips her hands inside the oven mitts. She carries the pot to the sink and pours water and spaghetti into a colander. "She's smart as a whip but struggles in social situations."

That word again. I'm *struggling*.

Dad runs his fingers through his hair. Around his temples are sprinkles of gray and even more in his trimmed beard. "She spends too much time on the Internet, finding diseases to worry about. I'm almost sorry I got her that computer."

*Hello. I'm here. Not eavesdropping from the living room.* Heat bubbles inside me. I sink my teeth into my lower lip, to keep from saying something that would get me in trouble. I don't care about Dad, but I think Mrs. Mac is trying to help me.

As if my thoughts have supernatural powers, Mrs. Mac hands the colander to Dad and turns to me. "I was packing up this evening and found a book for you, Kiara." She reaches for a stack of books on the kitchen table, but since she forgot to take off her oven mitts, she knocks them to the floor instead. She shakes her head, the same way she did in her driveway after the accident. "I'm sorry, dear. I'm getting so spacey."

"Maybe you hurt yourself this afternoon. I can look it up online," I offer, thinking of the search terms "concussion symptoms."

"No, it's everything. Not just today."

In my mind, I change the terms to "chronic disorientation"—some of the words I read last week when I was trying to figure out why Dad made the same thing every night for dinner, if he remembered to cook at all.

She ducks under the table. Her skirt spreads in a near-perfect circle across the wood plank floor. "Got it." She stands with the books gathered in her arms and gives me the one on top.

"*Animals in Translation*," I read, and then the author's name. "Temple Grandin." It's a grown-up book. A hardcover. The book's jacket is torn, maybe from falling off the table. Torn covers make me nervous, but I don't want to seem ungrateful. I try to make the edges stick together by rubbing them over and over with my fingernail. "Thank you, Mrs. Mac."

"She reminds me of you. And she has a special talent for understanding animals."

The X-Men have special powers, which is sort of like special talents except special powers are superhuman, like Rogue absorbing people's emotions, Karma making people go where she wants them to go using mental energy, or Wolverine healing tears and wounds. This Temple Grandin doesn't look like any of the X-Men. In fact, she looks like a grown-up cowboy with her Western shirt and square face. Her name could belong to a man too. I have to read the inside flap to find out she's a woman.

"Thank you," I say again.

Over dinner, Dad and Mrs. Mac decide to have her car towed to the junkyard and pay for the Elliotts' repair herself rather than calling her insurance company. Across the table, I finish the first chapter of the book. I have no special talent at understanding animals—in fact, the Mackenzies' cats and I pretty much avoided each other—but it's cool to read a book by someone who Mrs. Mac says is just like me. And she is.

Even though I started talking at a much earlier age than Temple Grandin did, she also got into fights at school and cried when people were mean to her. When she was going into ninth grade, her parents sent her to a special boarding school for emotionally disturbed children where she learned to talk to animals, like horses that had been mistreated. When I read that part, my stomach tightens up, and I can't eat anymore. I don't want to have to go to a special school. And I want friends who are people. Not horses. Anyway, Dad can't afford a horse.

I keep going because I know that if Temple Grandin wrote a book, she must have turned out all right. Dad doesn't tell me not to read at the dinner table. Mami would have, but she's not here. She hasn't even phoned us, even though Tuesday evening at six thirty is when she usually calls. After the plates are cleared—I'm too busy reading to see who does it—Dad says he's driving Mrs. Mac back to her new place with some of her boxes. "Go ahead and finish your homework," he says. "Ms. Latimer comes early on Wednesdays."

I fold a napkin in half to mark my place in the book. "Can you leave your phone?" I ask. "In case Mami calls."

He shakes his head. "She already called. When you were out."

"She called early?" *Unfair.*

"She has a rehearsal tonight. They're extending the tour."

"Which means she's not coming home next month?" My heart kicks against my rib cage. I squeeze the book, ready to throw it across the room. But what would Mrs. Mac say if I had a meltdown and destroyed the present she gave me?

"No, she isn't. She's touring all next month and then working at the studio through the summer." Dad rubs his eyes, then flattens his hair with his palms of his hands. "I don't like it any more than you do. But with your brothers in college and you going one day, we need the money." Glancing around the kitchen, I see that Mrs. Mac has left. Dad and I are by ourselves, and if he didn't have to take Mrs. Mac home, he'd go back into his pantry and play his songs the way he did when I got home this evening. The way he does every time Mami calls. Doesn't she realize how much we need *her*?

And I missed her call. Because I met Chad in the park, and we saw Mrs. Mac ram the back of his parents' van. He might be my friend now, but I have to do the right things so he won't go away like Melanie Prince-Parker and all the other New Kids.

I don't have Mami to tell me what the right things are.

But I do have Mr. Internet. And when I go upstairs to ask him how kids with Asperger's syndrome can find friends, he has 255,000 answers for me.

# CHAPTER 5

TEN MINUTES BEFORE ELEVEN, MS. LATIMER LEAVES. AND because it's another warm, sunny day, I go to the concrete platform in the park to read. Mrs. Mac's car is gone—last night I listened to the tow truck haul it away. The Elliotts' van, with its bashed-up back end, is still in the driveway.

The kindergarten bus pulls up between the park and the Elliotts' house just as I'm finishing the second chapter of *Animals in Translation*. Its brakes screech, driving a pair of robins from the bare branch overhead. A skinny boy with blond hair and a blue backpack jumps to the pavement. I recognize Chad's little brother from when they moved in three days ago.

"Hi, weird girl," he says when I wave. His grin reveals missing teeth on top.

I slam the book facedown on the platform. It has a torn cover, so it's already ruined. But now two pages are bent as well. "Is that what Chad calls me?"

The little boy skips up to me. "Yeah. He said you try too hard."

Teeth gritted, I snap at him, "So? I'm not supposed to try?" *How, then, am I supposed to make friends?*

The boy shrugs. "You don't have to be mean."

"Sorry," I mumble.

He holds out a grubby hand, palm up. "I'm Brandon."

"Hi, Brandon." I reach out to shake his hand.

"Slap it. Like this."

I give him an awkward high five that mainly catches his thumb.

"Want to play with me?" he asks. "I got wrestlers."

I don't want to play with a little kid. Chad's the one I want as a friend, even if he said I *try too hard*. "I'm busy. Reading." I hold the book in front of Brandon's face.

"Pretty please. Sugar on top." He pushes my book downward with pencil-eraser-size fingers and flashes his gummy smile. Freckles dot his little nose.

"Okay, okay. For a few minutes."

He dashes across the street and into his house. When he doesn't come out right away, I flip to chapter three, hoping that maybe he forgot or found something better to do. I get through a page and a half before he reappears holding a shoebox.

I groan. "Let me finish this page, okay?"

"Hurry up. You promised."

Inside the box are four-inch-tall plastic men, some naked to the waist, others with sleeveless shirts, all with oversize muscles. I set my book facedown on the platform, leaving animals behind for a little boy. Brandon leads me to the opposite corner of the park, where there's a children's playground with swings, a seesaw, and a pile of dirt in the place of what used to be a sandbox. We sit on the ground next to the dirt pile.

He hands me a wrestler. "The Miz," he says. He calls out other names as he pulls out figures. "Tatanka. Matt Hardy. The Rock. The Boogeyman."

I pick out an Asian-looking guy with lots of hair who wears a karate costume. "Who's this one?"

"Funaki. Tag team champion."

"I'm into X-Men. You heard of them?" I say.

"Nope."

"I got a bunch of comic books and stuff."

With the foot of one of his wrestlers, Brandon makes a lopsided circle in the dirt. I think of bringing over my figures. But I'm not supposed to mix X-Men with anything else because X-Men only go with each other—not with wrestlers or Power Rangers or Transformers. And I don't want to get them scratched or dirty.

"You can have a girl, 'cause you're a girl." He hands me a dark-skinned woman with black hair and a gray bodysuit. "That's Kristal. She's on the side of The Miz."

I turn her over. She doesn't look anything like Rogue. But I can pretend.

Brandon smacks two bare-chested figures together, grinds them into the dirt, slams one down onto the other one, all the while talking to himself. He uses some pretty nasty words too, words I don't expect a five- or six-year-old to know. Sitting next to him, I smell fertilizer—manure mixed with chemicals—and for a moment remember how Mami used to grow beans and tomatoes in our backyard, like her family did for generations in their small plot in El Salvador. My eyes are drawn to Brandon's ruler-straight hair, crookedly parted, roots crusted with grime. I wonder when he last took a bath.

"Let's make a ring," I say.

"Okay."

"Want to come with me to get a shovel?"

"I'm not 'lowed in anyone's house. I'm s'posed to stay here." He bites his lower lip.

"Then don't go anywhere. It'll only take a couple of minutes."

I take the shortcut through the fence, unlock the back door, and grab a trowel hanging from a peg on the basement wall. When I return, Brandon hasn't moved. He's a lot better at sitting still than his brother. I dig a dungeon-like ring with smooth walls and a flat floor. The soil is cool and damp, easy to dig and with a musty smell, cleaner than the smell that clings to Brandon. I pile the extra dirt and pat it down so Brandon's wrestlers can leap from the heights onto their helpless victims.

"Like my ring?" I ask.

"Yeah." One of his guys stomps another's head, over and over.

"Maybe your brother will be my friend now."

He doesn't answer but instead has one wrestler kick

another in the side of the face. The one kicked tumbles into the hole.

I pull a wrestler with a white vest from the box and make Kristal stomp him. Then I throw him aside and dance her around in a circle, shouting, "I win! I win!"

Brandon clutches my wrist. My body tenses. "No, that's not how you do it," he says.

"That's what you did."

"He's a good guy. She's bad. The good guys are s'posed to win."

"Then show me who's good and who's bad," I say.

Brandon lays the wrestlers side by side in two lines. He points to the line closest to him. "These are the good guys." Then the other line. "These are the bad guys." He picks up a pale man with black hair and a black vest and moves him from the bottom line to the top. "Last week he turned into a good guy."

"They can do that?"

"Yup," Brandon answers.

"No kidding!" I say. "So can the X-Men. Lots of them went from evil to good. Or from good to evil. Sometimes they went back and forth. There's this one, Rogue. She's me." Even though Brandon's gone back to bashing his wrestlers against each other, I describe how Rogue became a mutant from being exposed to toxic chemicals and how she started off with Mystique's Brotherhood of Evil Mutants because of the way people treated her. Then she found Professor X and older X-Men like

Wolverine and Iceman and learned to use her powers to help people.

I don't tell Brandon how Rogue asked Mystique to become her foster mother after her own mother left her—the way Mami did to me.

I lose track of time. The single dungeon becomes a chain of cells, some for matches to the death, others as hospitals for injured wrestlers or holding pens for those waiting to fight. Kids from the elementary school pass without noticing us. The middle-school bus squeals to a halt.

Three kids get off the bus, Chad first and then the twins Eddie and Mike Perez. Eddie and Mike push each other along the sidewalk next to the park. I hear one of them say, "Look who plays with babies," and the other laugh.

I ball up my fists, ready to chase them. I hear Ms. Latimer's words in my mind: *Count to ten. Think of something that makes you happy.*

Okay. I've spent three hours playing with a kindergartner and had fun.

My breathing slows. My fingers unclench. Chad walks slowly toward Brandon and me, his shoulders slumped. A breeze blows his hair away from his face to reveal a swollen, purplish-red left ear.

"What happened to your ear?" I ask.

Chad glares at me. "Bug bite."

Brandon stops playing and stares down at the wrestler in his hand. His lips move but no sound comes out. I wish I had the special power to read lips.

Chad taps his brother's shoulder. "Go on home."

"I'm playing," Brandon says.

"Get!" Chad drops loose wrestlers into the shoebox.

"Don't want to."

Now Chad pokes Brandon with the shoebox until he stands and clutches it to his chest. A single tear glistens on his cheek. Chad pushes him in the direction of their house.

"Why'd you do that?" I ask as soon as Brandon crosses the street.

Chad rummages through his backpack and pulls out a sheet of lined paper. "Here."

I read the note in neat cursive handwriting. *Dear Mr. and Mrs. Elliott: This is to inform you that your son, Chad, was disruptive in science class today. He refused to complete his assignment and wandered around the classroom instead. When I asked him to sit down, he ignored me. I sent him to the principal's office for the remainder of the period. Before he can come back to my class, I will need a parent's signature.*

I glance at the name. I didn't have her last year because I was in honors science and she taught the regular classes.

"Sign it."

"I'm . . . I'm not your parent."

"Duh." He takes out a spiral notebook and a pen. "Come on. Do it."

Now I realize why he needed to get rid of Brandon. "You want me to forge your parents' signatures?"

"Just my mother's. Or maybe my father's. But write something first so I can see what it looks like." He pushes the notebook toward me.

My hands stay at my sides. I've never forged anything before. Other kids forged notes to get out of PE, signatures on tests they failed, excuses for lateness. I never skipped class or failed tests. And you could get in a lot of trouble if they caught you.

But they can't catch me since they already kicked me out of school.

I see what Ms. Latimer calls a *win-win*. I get back at the school. And Chad will want to be my friend.

Brandon's words echo in my head: *He's a good guy. She's bad. The good guys are supposed to win.*

I'm not bad. I'm helping someone get out of trouble.

I take the pen and notebook and on the back cover sign my name in my jagged, tiny scrawl. I never could master cursive.

"Dad," he says. "You sign like my dad."

"Really?" I've heard no two signatures are exactly alike. Like no two genes are exactly alike.

"I thought it'd look like my mom's, you being a girl. And you have to make it bigger." He tears a page from inside the notebook. "Maybe you should practice."

"The teacher's going to know."

"How? I just moved here."

I point to the cardboard cover of his notebook, where I've signed my own name.

"Oh, yeah, right." He scratches out my signature and hands me the notebook with the torn-out page on top. "Sign it 'Chad H. Elliott. Senior.'"

"Senior?"

"Just 'S-R', okay?"

I take a deep breath and sign.

He lifts the page from my hand. "Bigger than that. And the 'E' like this." He makes a giant curly "E," so different from my blocky letter.

"I can't," I say.

"Then I'm hosed." He touches his ear, and I realize he doesn't have a bug bite. The skin on his ear is cut and a bruise is starting to form on the side of his cheek. He must have gotten into a fight at school, like I did. Maybe the school has already called his parents. This note would get him in even more trouble, and that makes me want to do an especially good job.

"Okay." I sign, imitating his loopy "E" so it's the biggest letter on the line.

"Perfect." He slips the note into his backpack and smiles at me. I think of Gambit smiling at Rogue as they battled the bad guys who mistreated them. Gambit wanted Rogue as a friend no matter how strange she was. If he really is like Gambit, this New Kid will stay my friend.

Chad sticks the toe of his sneaker into one of the holes I dug for the wrestlers. I tell him what I made—the dungeon ring, the hospital, the holding pen.

"Cool. I thought they were all jails," he says, adding after a moment, "Don't tell Brandon, but I'm getting him the Steel Cage Ring for his birthday."

"Isn't it expensive?"

"Yeah, it is, but I'm doing some things around the house."

"That's nice." Chad didn't intend to be mean to his

brother, but I bet he had to because of the note. I wonder why he got in trouble in the first place. It isn't that hard to sit in a seat, even in a boring class. "Why were you walking around?" I ask.

"Huh?" His mouth gapes.

"In class. To get you into trouble."

Chad shrugs. "I was itching."

"Bored?"

"No. Itching. Like I had to get up and move around. You know how it is?"

"Not really." I have no problem sitting still. I can do it for hours, reading or looking at the computer.

He spins in place. "I'm not passing anyway. I'll have to take this class all over again next year."

"No way." I think I'd quit school if they did that to me. "What if I help you? I had this stuff last year."

"It's too late." He skips from foot to foot as if he's itching again.

"Maybe not. You're in a new school."

He kicks the pile of dirt, destroying my hill. "Don't matter what school you're in if you're dumb."

I hope Chad's wrong. Because if he's right, that means it also doesn't matter what school you're in if you're weird.

# CHAPTER 6

"*HOW CAN I EXPLAIN PHOTOSYNTHESIS IF YOU'RE NOT EVEN* listening?" I ask Chad. I'm sitting on the concrete platform, his life science textbook open on my lap. Chad is spinning, one hand on the smooth trunk of a young oak planted between the path and the fence.

"You don't need to explain it. Just answer the questions," he pants, going around for the millionth time. How come he's not dizzy already? I feel light-headed watching him.

"She'll know it's not your handwriting."

"I'll copy it o-o-ver tonight." His feet make furrows in the grass next to the tree.

I slam the book shut, set it on the platform, and walk to the tree. Chad spins toward me. When he stops, he slaps his arms against his sides. I crouch and pluck a blade of grass.

"Photosynthesis. It's the process that makes grass turn green," I say, handing it to him. "Don't you ever wonder why stuff is the way it is?"

He flips his blond hair from his face. "Sometimes. Not school stuff."

"But you're not going to learn if I do your homework." For a moment, I consider writing out the answers for him. It would be so much easier. "The sun hits the trees and other plants."

Chad stands on one foot and looks up at the overcast sky. "There's no sun today. And it's gonna rain soon, so you better hurry."

"Okay, Chad. But sit down. You're distracting me."

"No. You sound like my teacher." Chad steps toward me.

I shrink away from him. "That's because I'm trying to teach you."

"How many times do I have to tell you? Just gimme the answers."

I suck in my breath. "Then what are you going to do for the test? Because I can't come in and take your tests for you."

"I'll figure out something."

"Do you want to *fail*?" That would be the worst thing. Everybody teased the kids who had to repeat the year.

"I hate you, Weird Girl." Little drops of spit come out with his words. He spins back to the tree.

I follow him, my vision blurred. If I do cry, he's going to start calling me Crybaby Kiara like all the other kids in school did. "I'm only trying to help. So you can pass."

Chad squints at me. "You know, you *are* that psycho eighth-grader! They say you cried every day."

I want to tell him: *Because people teased me every day.*

*And no one wanted to be my friend.* Instead, I brush the back of my hand across my eyes. "I'm supposed to be your friend. Right?"

"No," he says. "You promised you'd tutor me. So do my work or leave me alone."

I sputter, not expecting he'd say it like that, that he wouldn't want to be my friend either, after I tried so hard to help him. "Tutor means I explain it to you. Not do it for you. Like Ms. Latimer explains things to me."

"Go away!" Chad turns his back and runs toward his house, leaving his textbook on the platform. I grab it and follow him. By the time I get to his side of the street, he's already unlocked the door. But he's left both the outside door and the door to his house wide open, and I hear him call out, "Brandon, get outside! It's *your* turn."

I jump up the porch steps and step into the tiny entry-way. Before the door to Chad's apartment slams in my face, I notice his hallway filled with black garbage bags and a milky liquid leaking from one of them. Some of it has dried white on the gray linoleum. I don't smell milk, though, even spoiled milk. More like a thousand onions, concentrated into one super-onion.

I knock. No answer. "Chad, you left your science book in the park!" I shout through the door.

A woman yells from somewhere in the house, "Who did you bring here?"

"No one, Mom," Chad shouts back. "Brandon, out! Now!"

A minute later, Brandon opens the door a crack and squeezes through it. I step backward onto the porch and hand him Chad's textbook. He leans it against the wall in the entryway.

"Aren't you going to bring it to him?" I ask, worried that Mrs. Mac might think it's hers and take it away with the rest of her boxes.

"No," Brandon mumbles. He steps onto the porch. Fat raindrops pelt the ground. He looks up at me. "My mommy says you got to go home. Chad says you're bothering him."

"I was helping him. With his science homework," I explain, as if little Brandon would understand. And take my side.

"He don't want to play with you." Brandon shrugs. "I do, but it's raining. Wrestlers don't like to get wet."

The raindrops' patter quickens. Water streams into my eyes and down my cheeks. My hair hangs limp, soggy, defeated. If I hang around, I'll get soaked since no one's letting me in. This isn't Mr. Mac's store anymore. Blindly I stumble down the steps and dash across the street, through the park, to the gap in the fence.

I cross into my own yard, with its thick canopy of branches and the tire swing that makes me think of cypress trees over a bayou. If I were Rogue, the rain wouldn't bother me. I'd be used to it.

Dad isn't home from work yet, so I unlock the back door and go upstairs to my room, to my computer and Rogue.

I gaze into Rogue's glossy paper eyes and say out loud, "I blew it. Gambit's gone."

The rain falls in windblown sheets outside, and the thick clouds make it seem like dusk even though sunset is two hours away. I turn off the overhead light in my room and look out on the park and the Mackenzies' house where they don't live anymore. Water pours down the left side of the windowpane in a jagged triangle. Inside the triangle everything is clearer and larger, as if seen through a magnifying glass. I make out a small figure standing at the edge of the grass, next to the brand-new Nigel Mackenzie Park sign. He's put on a yellow slicker, but his face, the bottoms of his jeans, and his sneakers are soaking wet.

I can't get the picture out of my head: Brandon, in a little yellow slicker, standing by himself in the rain.

# CHAPTER 7

*IT RAINS FOR TWO DAYS STRAIGHT. I CLOSE MY BLINDS SO I* don't have to look at the park and think about my latest lost friend and his sweet little brother who plays with wrestlers. I catch up on the journal entries that I'm supposed to write for Ms. Latimer, which I write on the computer because she says she has trouble reading my handwriting. My printing isn't that messy, but it's teeny tiny and I use all capital letters because I want it to match the lettering of my comic books.

When it rains hard for a long time, that usually means a warm front is passing through—at least that's what Mr. Internet says. When the rain stops, the weather turns hot, record-setting hot for mid-April. I raise the blinds and open my window.

Music outside my window wakes me up early on Sunday morning. Not only Dad's guitar but new notes too. A banjo. The guitar and banjo carry on a conversation. Normally, I'd go back to sleep at eight thirty on a Sunday morning, but it's been a long time since I've heard music in the park.

I quickly get dressed, dash across my backyard, and slip through the fence. I recognize the skinny man playing banjo as Chad's father. The man who said they had no time for chitchat when they moved in last week. He and Dad are playing the song from the old movie *Deliverance,* the one where the guy with the guitar plays the riffs and the kid on the banjo repeats them. Dad nods in time to the rhythm and smiles while picking the notes of his turn. I smile too, listening to the lively tune so different from the sad melodies Dad plays in his pantry.

When the song ends, Dad looks up at me and over to the banjo man. "Chad, this is my daughter, Kiara. Kiara, meet Mr. Elliott."

Mr. Elliott holds out a weathered hand with brown-stained fingers. "Chad and Brandon's dad, right?" I say, hands frozen at my sides. Something about his fingers makes me not want to touch them. The stench of concentrated onions from black plastic garbage bags comes back to me.

Mr. Elliott gives me an open-mouthed grin. He's missing some teeth. Gray strands run through his ponytail like silken threads. There's stubble on his hollow cheeks and pointy chin. "Guilty," he answers.

I don't know what to say next. This is the guy whose signature I forged for my latest ex-friend. I sit on the concrete platform next to my father and wait for Dad to whisper to me not to be rude. I think of how Mami always warned me in Spanish, so most people wouldn't understand that she was letting me know I messed up. But Dad doesn't say anything. Instead, he hands his guitar to Mr. Elliott and takes the banjo from him.

At first, Dad's fingers are less confident on Mr. Elliott's banjo, but he seems to settle into playing an instrument with five rather than six strings. Mr. Elliott appears equally lost on Dad's guitar, which surprises me because Dad once told me the banjo is a harder instrument to play than the guitar. They play "John Henry," both of them singing along, neither winning any awards for vocals. Mr. Elliott's voice is gravelly and slightly off-key, Dad's thin and reedy, the result of the chemo they gave him for his cancer, which damaged his vocal cords. That's why Mami did all the singing.

After four more songs, they switch instruments again. Mr. Elliott lights a cigarette and leaves it between his lips, picking and smoking at the same time. "You play Béla Fleck?" he asks, the first thing they've said to each other since Dad introduced me. Dad nods and segues into the rhythm line of "Big Country." The sound of Mr. Elliott's three-fingered plucking sails over Dad's guitar chords. Several of his fingernails are missing, and I wonder how he can pluck the strings so fast with those damaged fingers.

I listen. The music makes me think of spring, buds bursting, leaves and flowers popping out in brilliant colors. I stand behind Dad and Mr. Elliott on the concrete stage, shuffle my feet, shake my hips, and finally spin in circles like Chad, my arms outstretched, letting the music vibrate throughout my body and the wind cool my face. I've left behind the confusing world of words.

After two more Béla Fleck songs, I sit, breathless from dancing. Dad checks his watch. "Time for breakfast." He taps my shoulder.

Even though I hate for the music to end and my real life to return, my mouth waters. Sunday morning before Dad goes to work is our special time. It was our special time even before Eli and Max went to college and Mami simply went. Dad would make pancakes from scratch with chocolate chips in the batter, more chips between each stacked pancake, and vanilla ice cream on top. He said it was our reward for all the traveling a family of musicians had to do.

Mr. Elliott sets his banjo on the platform and lights another cigarette. "Listen, I gotta ask a favor," he says, then adds, "Do you have any Sudafed? We ran out, and my little boy caught a cold."

*Duh. He was standing in the rain for hours on Thursday.*

"Sure." Dad glances at me. "Kiara, you know where the cold medicine is."

I bring back what's left in our box of cold medicine and hand it to Mr. Elliott. "I hope Brandon feels better soon," I say.

Mr. Elliott flips the blister pack up and down. "That all you have?"

"Sorry," I mumble, my eyes fixed on his fingers. The onion smell returns.

Mr. Elliott shoves the medicine into the back pocket of his stained and baggy jeans. "You were playing with Brandon last week, right?"

"Yes, sir." I stare at my own hands, smooth and perfect except for the bitten-down fingernails.

"He said he had fun. That you built a wrestling ring in the dirt."

"Yes, sir. It's over there. By the fence." I point to the mound of dirt in the corner next to the fence and the sidewalk. The two-day rainstorm filled in the holes and hollowed out my tidy walls.

"My other boy said he saw you too."

I nod, eyes again downcast, wondering how much Mr. Elliott knows about everything that happened last week.

"I'm going to send Little Chad over this afternoon. He got a new bike when we moved, and maybe you two can take a ride. Show him the town." He pauses. "You ride bikes, don't you?"

"I don't have one," I mumble, seeing my second chance with Chad slip away. Dad gave me a choice for my birthday. A bike or my own computer. No way we could afford both—even with his employee discount at Tech Town.

"Take Max's old bike," Dad calls out from the concrete platform.

I snap back, "It's rusted 'cause it got left out in the rain. It goes, like, two miles an hour if you pedal hard." And I know Chad isn't going to slow down for me. Not after he said he didn't want to be my friend.

"It didn't look rusted to me," Dad says.

"Did you ride it? No." After answering my own question, I say, "So don't tell me how Max's bike works if you don't know."

Dad turns away, as if I'd slapped him. And for a moment I wish I could have. I hate it when people tell me stuff that's not true, just to shut me up.

"If your mother were here . . ." Dad's voice trails off.

Heat rushes to my face. Eli and Max were right. If she were here, Mami would have talked to me—in Spanish so no one else could know that I ruined something. That I misbehaved in front of someone who Dad wanted as a friend, someone whose banjo chatted with his guitar in their special language that said, *We understand each other*, in a way that doesn't need words.

"No problem, J.T. We have an extra bike," Mr. Elliott says.

Dad returns his guitar to his case. I know *he* won't yell at me for whining and acting like a brat, but when we eat our pancakes in silence, it's going to be even worse.

# CHAPTER 8

**CHAD KNOCKS ON MY FRONT DOOR THAT AFTERNOON. "WANNA** ride bikes?" he says without enthusiasm. He points at the two red mountain bikes leaning against the tree in our yard.

I take a step backward. "I don't know. You were mean to me."

"My dad says you gotta show me around. 'Cause I'm new here and don't know where things are." His words don't match his tone of voice, and it makes me think he's not going to act nice if I do ride with him.

Still, I want another chance to be his friend—and to behave well for his father, since he's Dad's new friend. I messed up, complaining about Max's hand-me-down bike in front of Mr. Elliott, which made us look poor and Dad look like he didn't raise me right. After breakfast Dad apologized for not being able to buy me things other people have. He said that when Mami gets home with the money from her singing job, they'll buy me a new bike.

"Okay." I lock the front door and put the key on its

University of Vermont lanyard, around my neck. The lanyard was a birthday present from Max. I won't wear the BC lanyard Eli gave me.

The bikes gleam in the sunlight, inviting me for a ride. I run my hand along the shiny top bar of the smaller one. "These are, like, new."

"Yeah, we got them last week." He pats the seat of the one I touched. "This is mine. The other one is my mom's." I glance down and notice his mom's bike has the slanted bar, rather than the one straight across.

I ask him, "What makes you think I want to ride a girl's bike?"

"Because you're a girl."

"That's sexist."

"That's sexist," Chad repeats in a high-pitched voice. Mocking me already. He lifts his leg over the top bar of his bike. "Let's go."

I stand stiffly. "Not if you're going to make fun of me."

"Sor-ry." Chad bounces on his seat. "Coming or aren't you?"

Telling myself he sort of apologized, I push the girl's bike onto the sidewalk and slide on. Both bikes have a plastic shelf behind the seat and a pair of black saddlebags attached to the shelf. Some of our neighbors don't believe in cars, and this is how they go shopping. They tease Dad because he drives a crew cab pickup truck that uses a lot of gas. It would hurt my feelings, especially because I like his truck, but he just laughs and says, *When the band gets back together, I'll be ready.*

Signs reading NED LAMONT, U.S. SENATE have sprouted up amid the weeds and unraked, decomposing leaves in our old-hippie neighborhood. My yard's had one for two weeks, and when Chad and I turn onto busy Washington Avenue, I see one in front of his house. I figure Mrs. Mac put it there, but I ask Chad, "Your parents for Lamont?"

Chad doesn't answer, so I repeat the question.

He grunts. Maybe his parents don't vote. I tell him Mami isn't a U.S. citizen, so she can't vote, but Dad always took me with him to the polling place and let me pull the lever. "Straight Democratic ticket," I add.

"Where's the drugstore?" he asks, glancing back at me.

"What's that got to do with voting?"

"Nothing. I wasn't listening because you're boring." He slows down to let me catch up to him. "I need to buy cold medicine."

My lower lip trembles, and I quickly ask, "For Brandon?"

"Yeah."

"Okay, follow me." I lead Chad through the four-block downtown, past boarded-up shops and a new restaurant that was once a post office. On the block after the restaurant is a shabby drugstore with streaked windows and garbage on the sidewalk. We lock the bikes to a parking meter, sharing one meter and one lock. Chad takes a wad of bills from the side pocket of his cargo shorts and slaps a twenty and a five into my hand. For a moment, I stare at the bills. I don't get to hold much money these days, with the band broken up and the record store gone. I don't get to sell CDs after the concerts or stacks of old 33s and 45s in the store and impress the customers with my ability to calculate amounts in my head.

"You want *me* to buy it?" I ask, confused.

He nods. "They sometimes keep it behind the pharmacy counter. Buy as much as you can. And bring back the change."

"What about you?"

"I wait here. With the bikes."

*But he already locked the bikes. He doesn't need to watch them.* Still, I go into the drugstore alone. *If I do a good job, Chad will be nicer to me. He will want to be my friend.*

A musty odor greets me as soon as I pass through the door. The fluorescent lighting makes my eyes throb, and I hear buzzing overhead. I read the signs for the aisles. First Aid. Hair Care. Cold and Flu.

The shelves in the middle of the Cold and Flu aisle are bare except for a little handwritten sign. *For Sudafed, Contac, and generic pseudoephedrine, please see pharmacist.*

Just like Chad said.

On the back wall is the sign for the pharmacy, and I don't know why they would keep cold medicine behind the counter. All I know is that I'll have to look some grown-up in the eye and ask for it.

I wipe my sweaty palms on my jeans and force my shaky legs to take one step after another. Past the cough syrup and throat drops. Past the cookies, crackers, and potato chips in the next aisle.

A notice taped to the countertop says they only sell two boxes per person, and I have to sign a logbook. I ding the bell on the counter. The pharmacist is bald, with a mustache and square, rimless glasses. I glance into his eyes and say quickly before looking down, "Two boxes of Sudafed, please."

He hands me a clipboard and asks me for an ID.

"ID?" I had one for school, but now that I'm not in school, I don't carry it anymore. "I . . . I left it at home. Didn't know . . ."

"New law. Went into effect a while ago." He points to a blank line. "Sign it and remember next time."

I sign my name, pay for the medicine, and take the boxes out to Chad.

"Why didn't you tell me I needed an ID?" I ask him.

Chad shrugs and pushes open the glass door, leaving me waiting on the sidewalk. Wondering what this new law is and why it was passed. He returns with two more boxes, quickly unlocks the bikes, and wraps the chain around his seat. "Hurry up," he says. "We have to find another place."

"Another drugstore?" I ask as I lead Chad toward the river.

"Duh."

"But we have four boxes. Isn't that enough for Brandon?"

Chad seems to hesitate for a moment. "We're all going to catch it, you know."

The town park along the river has a paved bike path, and we ride next to the water, bits of sunlight flashing from the rippled water, wind blowing our hair in all directions. Chad and I turn right to get onto the bridge. I point out the four identical bronze statues of mermaids atop rocks, two at each end.

"The mermaid is the symbol of Willingham," I explain to Chad when we stop at a traffic light on the other side. "They say the early settlers drank too much ale when they went fishing, and they thought they saw mermaids swimming in the river."

Chad pushes his blond hair out of his eyes and stares at the river, as if mesmerized by its sparkling surface.

I add, "Some of the fishermen drowned when they dived in to catch a mermaid."

The light changes, and Chad says, "Skip the tour. Where's the drugstore?"

"That's the only one in Willingham. We have to go to College Park."

He groans. "How far?"

For once, I'm glad I've had to ride Max's beater bike around town because it's kept me in shape. "Couple of miles," I answer.

We cross the river and follow the state highway to College Park, the town next to Willingham, where the state university is. Cars whiz past, but the shoulder is wide, making it safe for us to ride one in front of the other. We pass a gas station, a Dunkin' Donuts, a highway overpass, and the large blue WELCOME TO COLLEGE PARK sign. A half mile later I point out the sledding hill and behind it the mountain bike trail where my brother Max used to ride with some of the College Park kids. At the sledding hill the

College Park kids wore expensive name-brand ski jackets with lift tags and acted like the place was only for them and not for us, but they always seemed to make an exception for Max.

"A good bike trail?" Chad asks.

"Yeah." I smile at Chad's first show of interest in any place I've mentioned to him, even though I've never been on the trail and wouldn't know a good trail from a bad one. "My brother says there's also a BMX track where kids do stunts."

"If we do this again . . ." Chad pants, his bike zigzagging on the uphill road that parallels the trail. I have to slow down not to leave him behind. "You gotta . . . take me . . . there."

I wish he said *when* instead of *if.* But at least he gives me a chance.

The shopping area of College Park has three drugstores, and only one of them keeps the Sudafed behind the counter. Chad and I split the stock on the shelves at the other two. I buy first, and he follows. Outside the last drugstore, we count our change and divide up six dollars and seventy cents, leaving three dollars and thirty-five cents apiece. We pack our boxes in the saddlebags—a total of twenty-four— and return to the store.

Chad runs to the magazine rack and lifts a copy of *Ride BMX* from the bottom shelf. On the cover is a picture of a boy with one of those helmets that covers the back of his head. He hangs in the air, legs outstretched, holding the handlebars of a bike that dangles beneath his body. Chad leafs through the pages, stopping to read from time to time, his lips moving slightly. I'm surprised to see him read, especially since I couldn't get him to look at his science textbook for more than fifteen seconds.

Farther down the aisle are the comic books. I leave Chad to his BMX riders and search the rows of *Iron Man*, *Spider-Man*, and—my heartbeat picks up as I draw closer to it—*X-Men*. I skim the one with Wolverine on the cover, looking for Rogue, but this time for Gambit too. *My Gambit has returned,* I tell myself. Maybe he'll be my friend since I helped him, just like I helped him when he needed his father's signature on that note from school.

Maybe I won't say something stupid to lose him this time.

Gambit appears in battle fighting alongside Rogue on one two-page spread, but most of the story is about Wolverine. That's okay with me. I like Wolverine too. He's strong and smart and knows his way. He was one of the first X-Men. He helped Rogue when she deserted Mystique's Brotherhood of Evil Mutants, haunted by the people whose minds she stole and who she left in a coma.

None of the other X-Men comics contains either Rogue or Gambit, so I take the issue with Wolverine to the register. Chad no longer stands next to the magazines, and I find him outside the door, tapping his foot on the sidewalk.

"About time," he says when I join him.

"Look what I got." I flip to the spread with Rogue and Gambit.

"Comics are dorky," he says.

"But this is X-Men." I point to the color drawing of Rogue. "Don't I look like her?"

Chad glances at the page and then at me. "Yeah." I think he's smiling, as if he really does like me now. Then he says, "She's kinda hot, though."

"And me?" The moment I hear my words, I realize what a dumb thing I said.

Chad shakes his head. "You're just a weird girl who reads comics."

He doesn't say it in a mean way, so I move my finger to Gambit. "This is you. Gambit. He's Rogue's best friend. I know he has brown hair and yours is blond so you don't look exactly alike, but he and Rogue come from the same place. She's from Mississippi and he's from New Orleans . . ."

Chad turns his back to me. He unlocks the bikes, fishes the boxes of Sudafed out of my saddlebags, and shoves them into his. "I was born in Iowa," I hear him mumble. "So unless they got one called Cornfield . . ."

I giggle even though he's making fun of the X-Men. "I'm not from Mississippi either. I'm from here. Well, Willingham." I tuck the comic book in the saddlebag.

But Chad has already jumped onto his bike and is pedaling toward home.

I catch up to him. Mami used to tell me I had to ask questions too so the other person won't think I'm boring and only want to talk about myself. That's how you make friends, she said. "So what did you buy? The magazine you were reading?"

"No." He pedals harder and shouts back at me, "Cigarettes."

I pull up alongside him again. "They're not supposed to sell them to you. That's illegal."

Chad laughs so hard he almost swerves into me.

I slap my forehead with my palm. Why would a drugstore sell things that cause cancer?

"What did you really get?" I ask.

In the seconds before he pulls ahead of me, Chad answers, "Baby Tylenol. For Brandon."

After I get home, I begin to doubt that twenty-four boxes of Sudafed, with twenty capsules each, are all for Brandon. That's 480 capsules total, enough for sixty people who caught a cold.

That night after dinner, when Dad thinks I'm doing my homework for Ms. Latimer, I ask Mr. Internet, *Why would someone buy 24 boxes of Sudafed?*

Mr. Internet's answer comes straight from the government. And it tells me why the drugstores are supposed to keep the boxes behind the pharmacy counter and make us sign for them and show ID: *"The United States Congress has recognized the use of pseudoephedrine in the illicit manufacture of methamphetamines."*

# CHAPTER 9

### *THE ELLIOTTS MANUFACTURE METH!*

So that's why Chad and Brandon stand in the park all day, even in the rain, and can't go home whenever they want. They're standing lookout in case the police show up.

As I read on, other details fall into place. Mr. Elliott's stained fingers. His rotting and missing teeth. The weird smells in the hallway.

Mr. Internet also tells me what I did all day long with Chad. It's called smurfing—going from drugstore to drugstore to collect the medicine that will be turned into meth once you pour a bunch of really nasty chemicals all over it. Muriatic acid. Anhydrous ammonia. Red phosphorus. Sulfuric acid. Stuff you find in Drano, industrial solvents, and fertilizer. Even the names of the chemicals are scary.

My hands shake so badly I can barely type the words into Google.

But I keep reading until I hear a knock at my bedroom door.

I let out a little shriek. It takes a couple of tries before I lock the little arrow onto the close button.

"Come in," I call to Dad.

"You screamed. Everything okay?"

"I was finishing my homework. You surprised me." In fact, I've done zero homework tonight.

"You look pale. Do you feel all right?"

"I'm kind of tired." I fake a yawn. "Chad and I rode all the way to College Park."

"Did you have a good time?"

I nod. I'm glad he didn't ask me about it at dinner. Instead he talked about jamming with Mr. Elliott, what a good time he had and how maybe they could play some folk festivals together this summer.

Now I don't know what to tell Dad.

*Your friend manufactures drugs.*

*The New Kid I wanted to be my friend manufactures drugs. He got me to help him—without telling me. And now my name's in two pharmacies' logbooks.*

But Dad and Mr. Elliott played such happy music together this morning. The music made my feet, my whole body dance. Dad's guitar and Mr. Elliott's banjo chatted with each other like friends sharing stories, and I didn't need the words to understand how they felt. Tonight Dad practiced those same songs, and they made me happy too. I danced all the way upstairs to Mr. Internet.

No, I can't tell Dad what the Elliotts are doing. I'll have to get them to quit doing it all by myself. Even though I couldn't help Chad with his science homework, I'll have to try harder. This time, I can't fail.

I have to be the superhero.


Ms. Latimer lets me get away with not finishing my homework *just this once*. And since I'm not paying attention—I couldn't get to sleep last night, turning over in my mind what I'd say to Chad—she leaves half an hour early. That gives me plenty of time to wait in the park for the middle-school bus.

The park is deserted before the bus arrives. Brandon, I imagine, is inside. Still sick. The Perez twins get off first, but they act like they don't see me. I stay in the shadow of the bus, not wanting to talk to them either. Chad steps off, waits for the bus to rumble away, and waves good-bye to Mike and Eddie.

Does he already have new friends? He's been here a week. New Kids don't hang out with me much longer than that.

He flips his hair from his eyes and walks toward his house, humming a tune and kicking stones on the way. Not noticing me. Yesterday, I was his friend because he could use me, but today I'm invisible.

"Hey, Chad," I call out.

He turns his head in my direction.

"I have to talk to you."

"Make it quick. I got stuff to do."

I meet him halfway, in the grass between the walkway and the sidewalk. Overhead, small, light green, and shiny leaves have started to break free from buds. My words have to break free too, but they've flown out of my head, leaving me standing mute like one of the dead branches.

"I . . . you . . . you used me yesterday," I begin. Not the voice, or the words, of a superhero.

"What are you talking about?" He shifts from one foot to another.

"I went online and found out what we were doing." My mouth is dry, and I can barely get the words out. "They call it smurfing."

Chad spits onto the ground, inches from my feet. "You don't know what you're talking about. You live on your computer. And in your stupid comic books."

"Were you really going to give Brandon four hundred and eighty pills?" I force myself to look into Chad's eyes. Pale blue irises, like a hazy sky.

Chad blinks. "What's it to you? I spent the day with you. My dad let you use our bike and bought you a comic book because your dad's a dirt-poor loser."

"No, he's not!" I scream. Heat rises to my face, to my ears, all the way down my arms to my fingers. My fingernails dig into my palms.

My vision blurs. I'm no longer a superhero. Evil mutant rage has seized me, the same rage that slammed my lunch tray into Melanie Prince-Parker's nose. My fist strikes Chad's chest.

He stumbles backward. "You're crazy!"

"I'm calling the cops."

"Don't you dare!" Chad is breathing hard, spit flying from his mouth. "We'll kill you and your dad. And no one will believe you anyway, 'cause you're psycho."

I charge him, head down. He steps to the side, and I trip over his foot and sprawl on the grass. He laughs. I jump up, swinging. My fist lands on his shoulder. His fist catches the side of my head, but I barely feel it.

I grab a handful of his hair. It's coarse, like bits of rope in my hand. He grabs my collar and his fingernails dig into the back of my neck. Our feet tangle, and we both fall to the grass, me on top of him. Hot breath whooshes past my face. I try to pin his wrists to the ground, but his skinny arms are stronger than I thought. He pushes me to the side, then rolls on top of me. I smell cinnamon and hear the pop of chewing gum. His body is solid and warm. Underneath it, I can't move.

I wriggle my right arm free. I lean to the left, pull my arm all the way back so that my elbow touches the grass, ball up my fist. With all my strength, I slam my fist against his bruised ear.

Chad screams and rolls off me. He rocks back and forth, covering his ear with his left hand, his screams turning to whimpers.

I stand and brush myself off, ready to celebrate my victory until I realize that I'm not going to become Chad's friend by beating him up. Nor will I get him and his parents to stop making meth by beating him up. In fact, his parents and the people they work with will probably come after Dad and me now.

If I don't make up with Chad right away, I'll make everything worse.

"Are you okay?" I ask. "I can bring you an ice pack."

Chad clears his throat. "I told Dad not to have me ride with you."

I rub my neck, where Chad scratched me. "I'm not stupid. I can figure things out."

"I know. But your dad told my dad you don't have any friends. So my dad thought . . ."

"I'd do anything to have a friend?" I clench my fists and Chad cringes, though the person I wish I could punch is my own father. Or Chad's father. Both of them got me into this. And anyway, both of them are right.

# CHAPTER 10

AFTER BEATING CHAD UP, I EXPECT NEVER TO SEE HIM AGAIN, but he rings my doorbell the next day after school. Both bikes lean against the tree in my front yard. And Chad has a bigger purple mark on his cheek where my fist landed.

"I'm not smurfing anymore," I say.

"We're only riding today. I wanna see that bike trail you told me about."

I stand in the doorway, speechless, my eyes fixed on the two shiny bikes in my yard.

Chad shifts from one foot to the other. "I'll be your friend, okay."

"For real?" My voice comes out as a squeak. "You're not just . . . using me?"

"Yeah." He waves me toward the yard. "Let's go."

One of Dad's happy songs plays in my head, fast-picked notes racing along with the major chords. The kind of song that makes me want to dance.

*Gambit's back. For real.*

I lock the door and roll the girl's bike away from the tree. It feels heavier than it did on Sunday, but once it's moving, I can't tell the difference. That's because of inertia, Newton's first law of motion. An object in motion will stay in motion. An object at rest will stay at rest unless acted on by a force.

On the way to the trail, I tell Chad, "You really are like Gambit. From the X-Men. Even if you don't come from New Orleans and don't have brown hair." Now that Chad has promised to be my friend, my mind and mouth are in unstoppable motion as I tell him everything about my heroes. He rides a little ahead of me, but I almost touch his saddlebag with my front wheel, close enough for him to hear me as we ride. "Gambit was adopted by a family of thieves who named him Remy LeBeau. They made him do stuff that was wrong and dangerous and against the law. Their bad stuff was stealing and gambling."

I pause to catch my breath. Chad twists his head back. "You done?"

I'm not. Chad needs to see where he fits in. "Gambit ended up running away from his family. Like Rogue ran away from home because her family wouldn't accept her, you know, being . . . different. Back before she took the name Rogue, when she was Anna Marie . . ."

Chad stands on his pedals, pumping hard, pulling farther ahead of me. I do the same to catch up to him. I'm about to tell him how Rogue and Gambit met when he says, "You want to be friends, right?"

"Yeah." I thought he already said he'd be my friend.

"I'm gonna give you some rules. Like you tutored me, I'm gonna tutor you." He slows down, out of breath from riding hard and talking at the same time. His bike wobbles a little. "Rule One. You don't beat up people you want to be your friend."

"I know." I lower my gaze to the cracked pavement of the shoulder.

"Rule Two. Nobody cares about the X-Men." He pauses. "Well, maybe other weird people like you."

I correct him. "Mutants. We're mutants. From exposure to toxic chemicals."

"Whatever. I'm not a mutant. I just want to . . ." His voice trails off. He swallows. "Grow up. Have fun."

I think about one of the things Rogue and Gambit had in common. "Have you ever thought about running away?"

"Can't," he says. "Can't leave Brandon."

Chad waves for me to pass. I don't want to get too far ahead of him, but it's also hard for me to ride as slowly as he rides on the uphill. Defying Newton's first law of motion, my bike drags and wobbles, and I have to pedal faster to keep it straight. I tell Chad to meet me at the right-hand corner with the Beresford Estates sign.

As I ride, I calculate how much older Chad is than Brandon. Seven years. The same as my oldest brother, Eli, and me. Eli's a crappy brother who's always called me the accident and thinks I shouldn't have been born, on account of what he learned in that premed class. Max is an okay brother—really into music and bikes. Sometimes he let me help him sample sounds for his keyboards when he played with the band. But he never looked out for me the way Chad seems to look out for Brandon.

Then again, when I was Brandon's age, it didn't matter. Mami was home. The band was together. Mr. and Mrs. Mac took care of me whenever my parents toured, and I went to school then. Even though the kids in kindergarten teased me for not talking or for talking funny, I didn't need a big brother to protect me. If I came home crying, Mami would sing to me. Or Dad would play a happy song. And if they weren't around, Mr. or Mrs. Mac would read me a story.

The Beresford Estates sign sits in a grassy patch that splits the street. When Chad gets to the corner, his face is bright red and beaded with sweat. "This it?" He points to the street of two-story houses, all with white siding and gray stone facades. "Look at those houses."

They're at least three times the size of my house.

"How many bedrooms you think they got?" Chad wipes his face with the front of his Patriots T-shirt.

"About two to a person," I answer. "My brother Max has friends from this neighborhood."

Three winding blocks from the entrance, the suburban street ends in a dirt road that slopes slightly downhill. I upshift, pedal hard, and feel the wind slap my face and the tires' bump-bump-bump through my entire body. Soon the open trail gives way to woods, and pine needles and rotting leaves cover the dirt. The leaves have a sickly odor, but I like the coolness of the woods after the long ride under the bare sun.

"Whee!" Chad sticks his legs out as he cruises. "This is fun!"

But then I see something at the end of the path. A fallen tree. A bicycle with a helmet dangling from one handlebar. And a guy with a chain saw. I squeeze the brake handles. "Slow down, Chad," I say. "We might have to go back."

Chad blows by me but comes to an abrupt stop in front of Chain Saw Guy. I slide off my seat and walk my bike toward him.

"Trail's blocked," he says. "Tree came down in the storm last week."

He looks about my brother Max's age, maybe a year or two younger, still in high school. His voice is deep, but his cheeks and chin are smooth, except for a few pimples above his jawbone. His wavy brown hair sticks up in spots and falls to the middle of his forehead. His skin is slightly tanned, a shade between Chad's pale skin and mine, which has the same color naturally that Dad has to go to the beach to get. The kid wears cargo shorts and a plaid shirt with the sleeves cut off, and on one of his muscular upper arms I see the tattoo of a guy on a bike and underneath it the word LIVESTRONG inside a yellow rectangle, made to resemble the bracelet. Black bicycle gloves cover his hands.

"Can we go around it?" Chad asks.

"You can help me clear it." The boy raises the chain saw.

"Sure." I lean my bike against a tree.

Chad reaches for my arm, but I pull away. "No. We have to keep riding. If we stop, we'll mess everything up," he whispers hoarsely.

"Mess what up?" I say out loud. Chad hadn't said he was in a hurry to get anywhere.

The older kid spins around, still holding the chain saw. "Yeah, what?"

"Nothing. We're leaving," Chad says. "Let's go."

My eyes lock on the older kid's tattoo and his muscles underneath. I came all the way over here and I want to help. I want to see the trail. "You asked me to show you here," I tell Chad.

"Yeah, but we can't stop riding. I . . . I have to get back." Chad shifts from one foot to the other, back and forth, like he has to pee.

"Go in the woods. We won't watch," I say.

He groans and glances up at the sky.

I lean toward him. "Do you have diarrhea?" I whisper. Despite all his fidgeting, he doesn't look like he has cramps.

"Yeah, diarrhea." He glances at the older kid and then turns away. Grabbing the handlebars, I roll my bike away from the tree. It would be embarrassing if Chad pooped his pants in front of this kid. When Chad flips his bike around, the back tire hits a root. I hear sloshing, a pop, and a sizzling sound. Not from Chad's innards. From a saddlebag. Chad swears. The kid jerks up straight.

"Wait a minute." The kid grabs the plastic shelf on the back of Chad's bike and pulls the bike toward him. He's a lot bigger and stronger than Chad is, and as long as Chad is giving me rules, Number Three should be, *Don't mess with the guy holding the chain saw.* "What's in those saddlebags?"

Chad struggles to keep his bike upright as it slides on the rotting leaves. "N-n-none of your b-b-business. I g-g-gotta take a d-dump."

"Do it in your pants, then." The kid laughs. I want to tell him how mean he's acting, but I know not to mess with Chain Saw Guy either.

The kid sets the chain saw on the ground, unsnaps the top of one of Chad's saddlebags, and peers inside.

"Stay out of there!" Chad screams. He lets go of his bike and shrinks back into the woods.

"Hmmm. Soda bottles," the kid says. He sticks his hand inside. "*Hot* soda bottles." He pulls out a clear two-liter bottle with the label ripped off and a churning white liquid inside, like the sizzling blood in my ears or the inside of an upset stomach.

Chad calls out, "Put that back!"

The kid carefully returns the bottle to the saddlebag and leans the bike against a tree. He walks toward me, leaves squishing under his sneakers. My mouth goes dry, and my insides churn like the contents of the bottle.

"Get away," he says. I back toward Chad in the woods. The kid draws from my saddlebag a green two-liter Mountain Dew bottle with the label still attached. "You the shake 'n' bake twins or what?"

Shake 'n' bake? What is that? My face turns hot, and my knees go weak. Could this be like smurfing? Did Chad lie when he said he wouldn't use me, when he promised to tutor me and be my friend?

"We . . . We're . . . l-leaving," Chad says. "Give us our bikes back, and you'll never see us again."

The kid puts the Mountain Dew bottle back in my saddlebag, steps slowly toward us as if he's thinking about what he's going to do, and grabs Chad's shoulder.

"Want to know how I know?" the kid asks.

Chad shakes his head. His hair flies into his face. His face is so pale even his lips have gone white.

I have no idea what shake 'n' bake means, except that Chad used me again to do something illegal and dangerous. But I have to save him, like Rogue swore to save Gambit. And by saving him, I'll escape too. "Let him go!" My voice squeaks, un-Rogue-like. I lower my gaze to the crumbly dark brown leaves at my feet.

"Leave the bikes here for now." The kid pushes Chad forward. "You too." He glares at me. Feet numb, I follow.

# CHAPTER 11

**THE KID LEADS US TO A NARROWER PATH OFF THE MAIN TRAIL** that ends in a clearing. The pine needle floor gives way to a bed of ashes surrounded by the charred trunks of young trees and a canopy of dead, bare branches, all black against the cloudless sky. The kid stops about ten feet from the ash and holds out his tattooed arm, keeping us behind him.

I suck in my breath. "Wow! A forest fire." I've never seen one this close up. Sometimes when the band traveled, we'd pass sections of forest that had burned. But then, we were going sixty-five miles an hour. Now I'm standing right in the middle of one. I step toward the ash.

"Get away from there," the kid says. "It's full of poison."

"What happened?" I ask. It doesn't smell like poison. Or a fire. Instead of the rotting-leaves odor of the rest of the woods, it doesn't smell like anything.

"You don't know?"

"N-no." It occurs to me that those bottles I didn't even know I was carrying might also be full of poison.

Sweat beads on Chad's face and his throat moves up and down, like he's about to throw up.

The kid folds his arms across his chest. I stare at his LIVESTRONG tattoo. His muscles. His tattoo again. "Six months ago, some loser was riding through the neighborhood on his mountain bike with a bunch of chemicals in two-liter bottles. Like yours."

"Wasn't me. I just moved here," Chad says.

"Didn't say it was. It was an older dude. Cops chased him in here. He crashed, a bottle busted open, and . . . *kaboom!*" The kid spreads his arms wide.

"Can t-these b-b-bottles b-b-blow up?" I ask.

"Yea-uh. Loser ended up in the hospital. Then in jail."

"You idiot." Chad glares at me. "Can you shut up? For once?"

"Don't talk to her like that." The kid pokes his finger into Chad's chest. Chad steps backward and almost trips on a root.

"She's retarded. She has nothing to do with this," he says, hands out in front of him as if to protect his already-bruised face.

I nod. "He told me he wanted to see the mountain bike trail. So I brought him here. He didn't tell me he had this . . . this *shake 'n' bake,* or whatever you call it, in the bags."

The kid approaches me, blocking my view of the ruined clearing. "What grade are you in?" he asks.

*Was* in. "Eighth," I answer.

He turns and looks Chad up and down. "And you?"

"Seventh." Chad stands up straight and pushes his shoulders back, as if trying to make himself taller.

"Okay, I get it," the kid says. "No one would think twice about kids on bikes. Cops wouldn't stop you."

"You're n-not g-going t-to call them?" A bead of sweat rolls down the side of Chad's face. And my knees are knocking together. It was bad enough when I got suspended from school. What will Dad say if I get arrested? Will I end up in reform school because I've already been in trouble?

A scream rushes up my throat. "Don't!"

The kid takes a step back and holds out his hands. "Whoa. Calm down."

But panic has seized my voice. "I can't go to juvie!"

"Why would *you* go to juvie?" The kid nods at Chad. "This little turd put you up to it. And whoever he works for."

"Don't call the cops, okay," Chad says quickly. "We'll leave."

"Wait a minute." He squints at me. I notice my UVM lanyard, twisted around my index finger, cutting off the circulation. My finger is swollen and red.

I shake my finger loose and rub it with my other hand.

"That a UVM thing around your neck?" the kid asks.

"Yeah," I mumble, eyes fixed on the ridges the lanyard cut into my skin. I wish he'd let us go because, like Chad said, we'll never come here again.

"Lemme see." The kid holds out his hand and adds, "I'm starting there this fall."

I take the lanyard from around my neck, key dangling from the end, and hand it to him. Now he knows I'm a latchkey kid wandering the town, getting into trouble . . .

But then he says, "Hey, I know you. You're Max's sister."

# CHAPTER 12

NOW I'M REALLY IN TROUBLE. MY LUNGS DEFLATE; HOT AIR rushes past my lips. I can barely get out the words. "Don't tell Max about this."

"Why would I?" the kid says. "Max would just love to hear that his little sister blew herself up doing something stupid."

"He . . . would?" My voice cracks. Of course. I'm the accident. The one who shouldn't have been born.

"No." The kid cuts off a laugh. "Big brothers don't like their younger sisters to blow up."

He gives me a funny expression. A smirk, which is supposed to mean he's joking about big brothers and younger sisters. But he hasn't told me whether or not he's going to rat me out to Max. Maybe if I'm extra nice to him, he'll let me go.

"So which of his friends are you?" I ask after a long moment. I don't recognize faces and have no memory for them, though I have a photographic memory of everything I read.

"Antonio. Trail name's Wheezer." He pulls an inhaler from the pocket of his cargo shorts. "For this, not the band."

"I'm Kiara," I say, my manners on automatic.

"Yeah, I know. Sure didn't expect I'd run into you like this."

I swallow the lump in my throat and dig my toe into the ground, defeated. Busted. I have nothing more to say. My gaze jumps to Antonio's wavy hair that falls over his forehead, to his brown leather necklace with a tooth pendant at his throat, to his shirt, unbuttoned to the middle of his chest, and lower, where he's tucked it into his jeans. His body is solid, pure muscle. The body of Wolverine. His gloved hands like Wolverine's retractable claws.

"How'd you get mixed up with"—Antonio jerks his thumb toward Chad—"that loser?"

Chad hides his face behind his hands.

"His family moved in across—"

"Don't tell him where I live, Kiara," Chad interrupts.

Antonio shoves his gloved hands into the pockets of his shorts. "Kid, what you and your people do is your business. Long as you don't mess up my backyard. But she's my amigo's baby sister, and I gotta look out for her."

"He told me he was my friend," I continue, trying to explain to Antonio how Chad and I ended up here together with four bottles' worth of chemical reactions.

Antonio touches his thumb to his own chest. The bare part, below the tooth pendant. "*I'm* your friend. He's trouble." He starts walking toward where we've left the bikes, staying close to me and far away from Chad. "You know, Max helped build this trail. It took about a dozen of us for the mountain bike trail and another dozen for the BMX track."

"I ride BMX," Chad calls out.

Antonio whirls around. "Did I ask you, dirtbag?"

Chad shrinks back, head lowered.

"It'd be cool if you could come here after school and work with us on the trail, Kiara. Keep up the family tradition," Antonio says. "I won't say anything to Max about the . . . the other thing, but I'll tell him you're helping out."

"Promise?" My muscles unclench as I see my way out. I'd never thought of my brothers' friends becoming my friends. They were just a bunch of guys who would hang out in our living room talking and laughing, and crowding our back-yard with their bikes.

"I promise," Antonio says.

I survey the path we take back to our bikes. This part is wide, but splitting off from it are narrow tracks carved out of the side of the hill. I can see why Max liked riding here and why Antonio got so mad at that guy who caused the explosion.

When we get to the tree where I left my bike, Antonio lifts the two bottles from my saddlebags. He holds one in each hand by its neck and moves in slow motion toward Chad's bike. There, he rearranges the bottles to fit upright rather than lying on their sides. He rolls my bike away from the tree and holds it out for me.

"You need to stay at least a hundred feet behind him." Antonio pats the seat. "In case he falls or runs into something and this stuff blows up."

"It only blows up if you open the cap," Chad mumbles.

"Yeah, right. Now get out of here and don't come back." Antonio picks up the chain saw and waves it in Chad's direction. "And keep away from Kiara. She doesn't need to be involved in your garbage."

I give Chad a head start and stay a hundred feet from him, as Antonio told me to do. Even though this part of the trail is a gentle uphill wide enough for two bikes, I worry with every little bump that Chad will wipe out and blow us both up. My sweaty palms make it hard to grip the handlebars. My mind returns to the bottles Antonio pulled from Chad's saddlebag and mine. Chad had promised to leave me out of his family's business, and he broke his promise. Like Gambit in the *X-Men* movie, he turned evil. He couldn't get away from his family's criminal activities even though he promised Rogue he would be her friend and join the X-Men. That's why I've always liked the comic books better than the movie. In the comics, Gambit was Rogue's friend and he was good.

I don't think Antonio will tell anyone about the bottles. And I believe him when he said he's my friend and Chad's trouble. *I'm done with Chad,* I tell myself. It's the first time I've ever dumped a New Kid. Antonio will be proud of me for doing it. But I'll have to figure out how to make Max's old bike get me all the way to College Park. I'll have to scrape off the rust so the bike looks nice, straighten out the brakes so they don't rub against the tires, and tighten the derailleurs so the gears shift like they're supposed to.

Antonio will be a better friend than Chad. He's way older,

like Wolverine. He's the kind of friend who'll protect me when other kids pick on me or take advantage of me. He won't make me do things that are wrong and dangerous.

Chad's bike wobbles on the uphill part of the trail. Right before the spot where the trail meets the road, he stops.

I don't want to stop for him. I don't want to ride anywhere near him. Cruising past him, I call out, "Meet me at the park for your bike."

He doesn't answer. Maybe he didn't hear me. I circle back to where he has stopped to rest.

"At the park. I'll give you back your bike."

Chad's head was lowered, but now he looks up at me. And then he screams, drowning out the birds in the trees, the distant whine of a leaf blower, the crunch of my bike tires.

He tugs at his hair. Strands cling to his fingers and fly loose into the air. I've never seen a boy pull out his hair before.

I spit out the words. "Why are *you* flipping out? You're the one that lied to me."

"Think I want to do this?" He gulps. "Our house stinks. Brandon's not getting better, and all they care about is their batches."

"But you said you wouldn't use me."

Chad covers his face with his hands. His entire body stiffens when he touches the bruise that I made worse yesterday. "Dad made me ride with you today. So I could carry more."

My stomach twists. I remember what he said yesterday right before I beat him up—about his parents and the people they work with, what they'll do if we try to stop them. *Don't you dare! We'll kill you and your dad.* They might hurt Antonio too.

Once again, I'm trapped. In a dungeon with no special powers to help me escape. Not knowing if beside me is evil Gambit or good Gambit.

"You're carrying four now just fine." He really isn't. He's wobbly and out of breath, but he shouldn't have lied to me and broken his promise.

"Yeah, I thought about leaving you behind and not telling him. But I wanted to ride the trail you told me about on Sunday. And see the BMX track 'cause I do freestyle."

"Freestyle?"

"BMX tricks. There was a big skate park where we used to live."

I point to his saddlebags. "You weren't going to do BMX tricks carrying this."

"Not today. I have another bike for BMX."

"So you brought me when you didn't have to so you could see bike trails?"

"Not exactly. You asked me to be your friend. So I was your friend. We were supposed to do fun things together."

"That wasn't fun. It was scary." Now I have to do what Antonio told me to do. I scrape the toe of my sneaker along the ground. "I can't ride with you anymore. I guess that means we can't be friends."

I turn the front wheel in the direction of the road, to leave Beresford Estates and Chad with his four bottles of chemicals.

"Kiara, don't go! Listen to me."

I try to push Chad's childlike voice from my mind. My tires bump onto the road.

"Please!" Chad's shout reaches me.

Maybe he really does want to be my friend. Nobody has ever begged to be friends with me. I let him catch up, even though I'm supposed to ride a hundred feet from him.

"You know what it's like," he says, voice small and choked. "Watching other people have fun and you can't."

"Because you're too weird," I add.

"Or your family makes you do things."

"Gambit's family."

This time, Chad doesn't warn me not to talk about the X-Men. Because he really is Gambit, and he needs me to help him escape.

If I agree to be Chad's friend and ride with him, he'll have to carry all four bottles by himself and my saddlebags will be empty. That's not the way friends are supposed to do things.

But if Antonio's really my friend, maybe he can help both of us, like Wolverine swooping in to rescue Gambit and Rogue from the families of criminals and the evil mutants.

# CHAPTER 13

*EXPECTING DAD TO BE IN THE KITCHEN OR IN HIS LITTLE* recording studio, I unlock the front door and tiptoe upstairs to my room. On the way, I listen for his music and sniff for the aroma of dinner. Nothing. I go into my room and bounce a few times on the bed before turning on the computer, making enough of a mess that he'll think I was in my room all along.

My stomach rumbles. All the bike riding and scary stuff have made me hungry. After finishing a page of social studies homework and watching the sunset from my window, I go downstairs.

The kitchen counter is bare. Dad leans against the back door, talking on his cell phone. I strain to hear what he says and if he's talking to Mami. It's Tuesday night, her usual night to call, but she already called on Sunday night this week. She didn't say she was coming home.

"If I can get off work, I'll come to New York . . . I'd like to get something started again." Definitely not Mami. He turns his back. I expect him to say something about me. "Money's tight. I have to get paid . . . Twenty bucks playing in the subway isn't going to cut it."

Nothing about me. He doesn't even notice me. And he didn't mention me, only that he's trying to *get off work* to go to New York. What does he plan to do with me? Take me to New York to pass around a bucket on the subway while he plays?

Dad snaps his cell phone shut. I wait for him to turn around, but he stands frozen by the door, staring through the dark windowpane into the backyard. I know he can't see anything with the kitchen light on except his own reflection. That's what I see from the other end of the room—his reflection and above his shoulder, a tiny me.

"Where's dinner?" I ask, breaking the silence.

He jumps. "Oh, hi there." Not exactly the *where were you?* I expected.

"I'm hungry."

He opens the refrigerator to reveal a bag of wilted lettuce, a carton of milk, and mostly empty shelves.

"That's it?" *Don't push it,* I tell myself. *You were the one who disappeared all afternoon. Doing bad stuff too.* But this time I can't stop myself. My blood thumps in my ears. "Are we so poor we can't afford groceries? Or you just don't care?"

His eyes slice through me. I look away. "Maybe we should order a pizza," he says.

"Mexican. We had pizza last night. You picked it up in Manchester after work." I tap my fist on the edge of the counter, in time to the beat inside my skull. "The pizza in Willingham stinks."

He flips open his cell phone. "Garcia's doesn't deliver, and I'm too tired to drive there."

"I want Mexican!" I pound my fist on the counter as I repeat the words. The countertop is shaking—or is it me? I want to bang my head against the counter like I used to do when I was younger, because maybe if I bang my head hard enough, I'll set free the thought that Chad tricked me into doing something evil and scary and my father didn't even notice I had gone. And that when I came to the kitchen wanting dinner, he didn't see me because I was invisible and the person on the phone was real.

"You're too old to be throwing tantrums," Dad says in his truck on the way to Garcia's in College Park.

"I know. I'm sorry," I mumble. I'm also too old to play with X-Men figures and kindergartners and to cry every time someone's mean to me or things don't go my way. But so far, Mr. Internet hasn't given me any rules on how to stop.

"Think about what made you melt down tonight," Dad says. "I'm sure it wasn't the bad local pizza."

I rub my aching hand. "You forgot about me. You always tell me not to interrupt, so I didn't interrupt and you acted like I didn't exist."

I examine the pink mark on my fist that will be a bruise

tomorrow, but out of the corner of my eye, I see him nod. "I should have noticed sooner. And praised you for not interrupting. But it was an important call."

My stomach twists. *Important call* usually means change, and not in a good way. "Who were you talking to?"

"He's an old friend in New York City. Someone I used to play with. We're trying to get into some summer festivals."

"What'll you do with me?"

He hesitates for a long moment. "Bring you along. And your brothers too, if they're free." His eyes are on the road. Not on me.

I sniff. "Just don't leave me with them."

"Why? You've stayed with Eli and Max before."

"I'm scared of Eli."

Dad's hands tighten on the steering wheel. "What happened?"

"I heard Eli say something to Max . . ."

"You know they don't mean it when they call you the accident."

"Except that I was." I clench my uninjured fist. The other will only bend partway. "Why did you and Mami have me when you knew I'd be . . ." I spit out the last word. "Defective?"

He reaches toward me. I shrink away, press myself against the door. Rogue cannot touch or be touched. "You're not defective, Kiara. You lost your temper and got into trouble at school. Ms. Latimer and I think it's . . ." He takes a deep breath. "Nigel's death. Dee moving away. Your mother leaving. Too much . . . stress for you."

"That's not what Mrs. Mac said." I can't believe it was only a week ago, when she told him the same things I'm telling him and he made the same excuses. "She gave me that book by someone who's like me."

"I agree that Dee's trying to help, but—"

"What about in kindergarten, when I didn't talk for six months? That's one of the signs, you know." Before then, I'd sing entire songs from TV in English and Spanish, and everybody thought I was a genius. But when I started talking again, my voice was funny. Off-key. Flat. And I had trouble pronouncing all the big words I knew. "What about . . . ?" I stop.

Suddenly, I don't want to talk about it. The teasing. The kids who beat me up and the ones I beat up. Katie Lyon in kindergarten. Sammy Ortiz in second grade. Jason Karl in fifth. Emily Stein in sixth. Melanie Prince-Parker in March. And Chad yesterday. My face feels hot and damp, but when I think of some of the kids I gave it back to, I smile.

Then I remember the last birthday party I went to, and my smile fades.

Fourth grade. Emily Stein.

We weren't friends, but her mother took Spanish lessons from Mami. Mami bought me a new puffy-sleeved dress with seams that stuck out on the inside, and it itched like crazy. In the car, I chewed on one of the sleeves to take my mind off the itching.

At Emily's house, I sat in a corner of the living room and kept chewing because none of the girls talked to me. When they lined up for Pin the Tail on the Donkey, I got in line too because the winner was supposed to get a prize.

"The back of the line is that way, Kiara." Emily pointed to where I'd been sitting.

"No, it's not," I said, because I hadn't cut in line. I saw no one in back of me.

"Emily's right," one of her friends said.

Another girl joined in. "You have to wait your turn. Like the teacher always says."

"You're just making me sit down again. You don't want me to play." They never did. At school they always said they had enough people when I tried to get into the jump rope line or their kickball games.

Emily whispered to her friend, but loud enough that everyone could hear her. Including me. "I didn't want to invite her. But I had to. On account of her mom teaching my mom Spanish."

My eyes watered, and my cheeks stung.

"Look, she's crying again," someone said.

Quickly I wiped my face on my sleeve. My upper arm felt damp, and I didn't have to look to know why.

"Hey, there's a big hole in her sleeve."

"She was chewing her dress."

"Yuck!"

"Like a billy goat."

One of them poked her finger through the hole and touched my arm. I trembled, then let out a scream. The film over my eyes cleared, and I saw not the girls but the table where the birthday cake sat. It had green icing and a maypole with little figures dancing around it. All the figures in one happy circle. No one left out.

I ran to the table with the maypole cake and flipped it over.

*Never invite Crybaby Kiara to your birthday party, or you'll be really, really sorry.* For the next two years, Emily and her friends told everyone so and the reason why. Because of her I never got invited to another party again. Which was why I had to yank out a handful of her frizzy brown hair and bloody her lip one morning before school, while all her mean friends tried to pull me away.

Dad's no longer driving. He turned off the road somewhere and cut the engine, and now he holds me in the still, dark truck cab, his arms squeezing my shoulders, his soft beard against my forehead.

"You got cured, but there's no cure for what I have," I say.

And I finally tell him what Mr. Internet told me about Asperger's syndrome, that it's not something you can take a pill for. "It's probably genetic. You weren't supposed to have any more kids."

In my mind, my genes are a giant twisty ladder—two parallel strands connected by crosstrees—the way Mr. Internet showed me. Sometimes they're red, blue, green, and yellow—colorful and pretty. Sometimes they're dark and ugly. Mine are always broken—strands bent and crosstrees knocked out. That's what poison chemicals do. Dad's broken genes making broken copies.

"What exactly did your brothers say?" Dad's voice is hard, like he plans to get both of them in trouble.

"Just Eli." I don't want Max in trouble for nothing. Especially now that I know he's Antonio's friend. "He learned about it in one of his classes. That the chemicals they gave you to get rid of the cancer cause genetic mutations."

A couple of cars pass by our parked truck, their headlights turning everything inside shadow and silver. "I'm sure Eli thinks he knows everything now that he's in that premed program. But there's no proof that what they gave me causes birth defects." Dad's chest rises and falls against my upper arm. "At least once the treatments are done."

I swallow the knot in my throat. Eli had a special class about all this stuff. He should know. Dad quit college in his sophomore year and said he cut most of his classes before then to play music or do what he called *solidarity work*. Mami's smart, but she probably couldn't understand the doctor because she doesn't speak much English. "Whatever. At least you guys wanted me." I swallow again. "Just don't change your mind on account of what you got."

Dad squeezes me tighter. Any more, and my eyes will pop out. "Never."

"What about Mami?"

"Your mother loves you."

"Then why did she leave me?"

Dad releases me from his death grip. "She has to make a

living, which she can do in Montreal but can't do here. More than anything, she misses you."

I fold my arms against my chest. "If she misses me so much, she should come home."

I wish Dad wouldn't keep talking about Mami at dinner, but he does, even if what he mainly talks about is how Garcia's isn't real Mexican food and how Mexican food is different from Salvadoran food. It makes me miss Mami's *pupusas,* thick tortillas filled with beans or cheese and served with tomato sauce and pickled cabbage called *curtido.*

"You still love Mami, right?" I ask him on the way home.

He nods but doesn't say anything.

"And she still loves you, right?" When they first met, he didn't speak Spanish, and she barely spoke English, and they didn't seem to learn much of each other's language over the years. Sometimes when Mami got mad at Dad, she'd yell at him in Spanish and English and he'd sit there quietly as if he didn't understand either language. But whenever they played music together, I could tell right away that they loved each other. They didn't need words— the music said everything.

"If your mother could be here with us, she would," Dad finally says.

I don't think he wants to hear me tell him how in *X-treme X-Men,* Rogue left Gambit even though they loved each other because she had to kill the evil Vargas, who had attacked them. Gambit almost died while Rogue was gone, but she got back just in time to save him. Once right after Mami left, he yelled at me because I talked about nothing but X-Men, so I imagined myself writing a sticky note saying, *Never talk to Dad about X-Men* and slapping it inside my brain.

# CHAPTER 14

*I DON'T SEE BRANDON OR CHAD GET OFF THE SCHOOL BUS*
the rest of the week. I watch for them through the hole
in the fence as I work on Max's old bike using the directions Mr. Internet gave me. I sand the rust from the frame,
crankset, and cassette; tighten the cables; straighten the
brakes; clean and oil the chain; and inflate the tires. Now
that I'm five foot four, the bike fits me perfectly. It's heavier
and harder to pedal than Mrs. Elliott's bike, but it will get
me to College Park. On Thursday, I ride to the pharmacy in
Willingham to buy black nail polish. The lady at the register stares at me, and I look away. I think she remembers
me from when I bought the Sudafed and now believes I'm
one of those creepy druggies who dresses all in black and
paints her fingernails and toenails black too.

On my way back home, I see Brandon standing next to
the concrete platform in the park. He clutches the edge of
the platform and doubles over, coughing.

I ride up to him. "You okay?"

Brandon gasps for breath. His mouth looks like that of a fish taken out of the water. "Chad . . . says . . . I got . . . puny-monia."

I laugh at the way Brandon says it, even though it's not funny that he's so sick. "It's pronounced *new*-monia."

"*New*-monia," he repeats.

"Is Chad sick too? I haven't seen him."

"He said he was getting medicine. But he ain't back yet."

Brandon coughs again. I hear him sucking mucus into the back of his throat. "You shouldn't be out here if you're sick. You should be in bed," I tell him.

"Mommy says I need fresh air."

*Or to stand lookout.* Which means they're cooking at home again. Are they still making Chad carry the bottles too?

Friday it rains. Before I have a chance to take my bike to the trail Saturday morning, Chad shows up with his mountain bike and a scratched BMX bike.

The bruise on his cheek is faded. But he has a scrape on his forehead.

"Maybe you should wear a helmet. Those bikes can be dangerous." I point to his BMX bike and think of the pictures in that *Ride BMX* magazine he was reading in the drugstore. Everyone in the pictures had a helmet because it's easy to fall doing tricks and crack your head open. "We have a helmet you can use."

Max left his old helmet in the lean-to, and he's at college, so he won't mind if I loan it to Chad. I run through the house and out the back door. Max's helmet is balanced upside down on a ladder and covered in cobwebs. I wipe the helmet on my jeans. Strands of spiderweb cling to my thumb and forefinger.

When I return, Chad has leaned his mountain bike against the tree. He sits on the BMX bike, rolling it back and forth. "Here," I say, holding the silver helmet out to him.

Chad pops a wheelie. "I'm not taking your crummy helmet. You wear it."

Cobwebs still crisscross the inside, and dust coats the felt pads. "Yuck." I set the helmet on the top step, by the front door. I figure I can clean it before I ride to College Park. "Want to show me some tricks?" I ask Chad.

Chad walks the front wheel in a semicircle. "No. I want you to talk to your friend about letting me ride on his track."

"M-my friend?" I stammer. Antonio said that he's my friend—and that Chad's trouble. But my stuck tongue tells me I don't really know what Chad is, and I'm not sure Antonio's enough of a friend that I can ask him.

Chad pivots to face his mountain bike. "You can ride the boy's bike."

My mouth goes dry. "I'm not carrying your . . ."

"I don't got any. See for yourself."

I approach the mountain bike as if it were a bomb, slide my fingers into a saddlebag, wriggle them around. Nothing but warm air. The same with the other bag. "So you just want me to talk to Antonio?"

"Yeah. But I gotta make a stop first. You don't have to go in."

One stop turns out to be all the drugstores in College Park. One of those that kept Sudafed on the shelf last Sunday now locks it behind the pharmacy counter, Chad tells me. And the other one only has three boxes. Chad limps a little when he goes inside, and when he comes out almost empty-handed, his face is pale. The three boxes fit inside the pocket of his cargo shorts.

We ride to the bike trails, my stomach tightening the closer we get. Will Antonio tell Max if I bring Chad back—even though Chad doesn't have any dangerous chemicals on him?

All this is so new for me. I know what it's like to be excluded, to have no friends. I don't know what it's like to be invited and then have a friend who I'm trying to get invited too. "What do you want me to tell Antonio?" I ask Chad, because he's supposed to be my tutor in these things.

He rolls his eyes toward the sky and says, "I'm doomed."

*Because you don't think I can do a good job?* Swallowing hard, I pass Chad and turn into Beresford Estates without a backward glance. I'll show him I can talk to Antonio. I don't need any help.

The damp ground smell, mixed with pine sap, hits me as soon as I enter the canopy of trees. My tires kick up mud that pelts my ankles where I've rolled up my pant legs. The tree that blocked the path has been cleared and the trail stretches out ahead of me. I pass the sawed-off trunk of the fallen tree with only the briefest glance at its exposed rings. The trunk is the diameter of a basketball. The tree had many years ahead of it.

"Beep, beep," Chad calls from behind. I veer to the right, and he pulls even with me on the wide trail.

"Maybe he's not here," I say, disappointment muffling my voice.

"Then we ride until we find it." He lifts the front end of his bike and leans backward slightly so he rides only on his rear tire.

"How did you do that?" I ask when his front tire returns to the trail.

He doesn't answer. I know the answer anyway. Lots of practice. A few scrapes and bruises.

Chad and I ride alongside each other into the maze of trails. Even if we get lost, I figure we'll find the BMX track eventually.

The main trail, wide enough for our two bikes, splits into three trails, each one narrow and twisty. The first one we take dips and rises before it leads us right back to where we started. We then take the third trail, which crosses a creek twice, once over a bridge, the other splashing through the water. After following the creek for a while, we head back uphill. I pass Chad because his BMX bike doesn't have low gears. Rotting leaves and pine needles cover most of the trail, but near the top of the uphill part, we hit sand that makes my bike fishtail.

We emerge from the sandy section at the bottom of a grassy hill. Chad stops. He leans against the handlebars, panting, clutching his right side. His eyes are squeezed shut. Faint voices, voices of older boys, rise from the other side of the hill. My stomach does a quarter turn. If Antonio is here . . . What am I supposed to say to him? What would Rogue tell Wolverine so he'd let Gambit join the X-Men?

Laying my bike on the ground, I climb the hill. When I get to the top, I see an open area with BMX bike jumps made of sand, tires, and plywood. The meadow surrounding it slopes gently upward to more woods. I stand at the only steep side, but the entire BMX track appears carved out of the meadow below.

I gape at the massive sandbox that makes real people appear as small as action figures. Antonio isn't there, but two other boys wearing helmets ride on separate mounds, and a bigger kid with sideburns sits next to a wheelbarrow. He holds a video camera.

I scoot back down the hill before they see me. "I found the track, but Antonio's not there," I whisper.

"Good. I'm riding," Chad says. He pushes his bike up the hill. I leave mine at the bottom and follow, feet dragging, certain that if Antonio isn't there, the others will kick us out.

Chad stumbles once on the way up. But at the top he waves, yells, "Look out!" and flies down the hill into the pit.

He zips up a mound, catapults straight into the air, and turns 360 degrees—twice—before riding down the other side of the mound. I suck in my breath.

"Did you see that?" a biker shouts.

"What?" The kid with the camera stands and whirls around.

"You missed a double 360. All the way from the peak." The first kid turns to Chad. "Who are you?"

Instead of answering, Chad circles the pit, climbs the mound again, and makes a three-quarter turn in the air. His long blond hair flies out around him. The three other boys stand in a clump, watching. They ask him where he learned to ride like that.

"Around," he answers. The trick he did for me is nothing compared to the ones he shows those kids. The one with the sideburns lifts the video camera to eye level. Recording Chad.

Ignoring me.

I stand at the top of the hill, invisible again.

The BMX track is just another lunchroom table where New Kid has found his group of friends and left me by myself. I feel like crying, but if I do, all three of these boys will also know I'm Crybaby Kiara.

So I call out to Chad, "I have to go. I'll leave the bike in my backyard."

I don't think he hears me.

# CHAPTER 15

CHAD NEVER COMES TO PICK UP THE BIKE. I SEE HIM IN THE afternoon, limping along the perimeter of the park, hunched over, head down.

He probably wiped out, the crazy way he was riding. *Serves you right for pretending I'm not there,* I want to tell him. Instead I lower the blinds.

A distant banjo and guitar greet me when I wake up the next morning. Outside, Dad and Mr. Elliott are playing again. After getting dressed, I roll Chad's bike from under the lean-to, through the gate, and around the block into the park. I'm going to return it because he didn't pick it up and I don't need him or his bike. I can ride Max's bike to meet Antonio.

Much as I wish I could stay and listen to the music, I can't because I might say something to get Dad and me hurt or killed. Like, *How could you think I was so desperate for a friend that I would break the law and put myself in danger?* So when they stop for a break, I push the bike forward and mumble, "Chad left this at my house."

"Speak up, girl," Mr. Elliott says.

"Chad. Left. This."

Dad glares at me. I don't care. Mr. Elliott doesn't deserve my good manners.

He sets his banjo on the platform, grabs the handlebars, and leans the bike against the concrete. "Is she your only one, J.T.?"

"No, I got two boys—Eli and Max. Both of them at college." Dad sets his guitar next to the banjo.

Mr. Elliott holds out his hand, with its stained fingers. "Got pictures?"

Dad takes his wallet from his back pocket. The top photo is of all five of us together, before Eli, Max, and Mami left. I was around ten then, and both Mami and I wore embroidered peasant-style blouses. My hair came to my shoulders and curled under my chin. There was a gap between my teeth. I wore braces all through sixth grade to get rid of it.

Dad digs under the photo for more, but before he can take them out, Mr. Elliott lifts the wallet from his hand for a closer look. He then pulls his wallet from his pocket and hands a worn photo to my father.

"Here's Lissa with baby Brandon. He was a real sweetie." Mr. Elliott taps the photo with the corner of Dad's wallet. "The other one busted our chops from day one. Colic. Wouldn't sleep . . ." I peer over Dad's shoulder at a skinny woman, her long straight hair parted in the middle, holding a smiling, round, bald baby in her lap. She's smiling too, her thin lips pressed together. Baby Brandon has a pair of teeth on top that glisten like tiny pearls.

Dad has photos of all of us. Mr. Elliott has the one with Brandon and his mother and another of Brandon that looks like it was taken at the hospital, with him all red and wrinkled and wearing a blue knit cap. Nothing of Chad. Even though I'm mad at him for ignoring me and hanging out with the older boys, I wonder what he looked like as a little kid, if he looked like Brandon does now—sweet and innocent rather than hard and mean.

Dad and Mr. Elliott are still looking at family photos when I go back inside. I drag Max's bike outside, ready to go. Chad has made his own friends at the BMX track. I don't have to ask Antonio to let him ride there. But Antonio did say he wanted me to return to the trail—he just didn't show up yesterday. Remembering that kid with the sideburns and the video camera, I get an idea. If I record the stunts, maybe they'll notice me, talk to me, want me to stick around.

Dad keeps our video camera in his tiny recording studio. He bought it a little over a year ago, and I used it to record Corazón del Este's concerts. Most of the time, I'd set the camera up on a tripod and let it run. Sometimes I took handheld footage, getting right in front of the musicians or sneaking backstage to shoot them from behind, which was my favorite because it sort of made me part of the band too.

I posted the videos on YouTube—Dad's idea to get more people to hire us. We got over a thousand views in all and a few people left thumbs-ups. When someone wrote, *Nice-looking band. Great costumes,* I ran bragging to everyone in my family because it was hard to get the colorful outfits they performed in to stand out with the bad lighting. But even though the band looked good, Mami said we didn't get enough gigs to pay the cost of the camera, even with Dad's employee discount at Tech Town.

I wait until after breakfast, when Dad leaves for work. Then I put the camera into my backpack and ride to College Park.

Like yesterday, the mountain bike trail is deserted. The extra day of sunshine has chased away the musty smell, but the breeze makes me shiver where the trees block out the sun. I think about turning back. Antonio never gave me his phone number. Maybe he didn't mean it when he said he wanted to see me again . . .

"Hey, Max's sister! Like your bike."

Antonio rides downhill toward me on the trail next to the creek. Even with his helmet on, I recognize the solid jaw, the skin almost as dark as mine. I squeeze my brakes and glide to a stop on the bridge.

He stops at the edge of the creek just before the bridge, lifts his leg over the bar, and slides to the ground. His face glistens with sweat. Today he wears a long-sleeved shirt, but with the sleeves rolled up to the middle of his forearms.

"I fixed it up," I say.

He strips off his gloves and runs his finger along the top bar, stopping at the bumps where I sanded and repainted the frame. "Nice job. What did you use for paint?"

"Nail polish. Looked it up on the Internet."

"I guess you can get away with buying that stuff easier than I can," he says.

I swallow the tightness in my throat. "Where were you yesterday?"

"You stopped by?"

"Yeah." I say nothing about Chad.

"I had a race down in Mystic."

I examine Antonio's bike up close. Its metallic red paint is nicked and dulled, but the bike is way fancier than Chad's, with shock absorbers underneath the seat as well as on the front fork. The wheel rims are black rather than chrome. It's the kind of bike someone would use for racing. "How did you do?"

"Not so good. Fourth. I was in the lead until my asthma kicked up." He clears his throat. "I'm taking it easy today. Still hurtin'."

I wish I could touch him, help him feel better, but I keep my hands on my bike. *I'm not Rogue,* I tell myself. *I won't suck out his emotions if I touch him.*

I step backward, stumble over a root, and plant my foot in the creek. Cold water rushes over the top of my canvas high-tops. Antonio grabs my upper arm to steady me. I stiffen.

"You okay?" He lets go.

I pull my foot onto the bank. Water streams toward the creek, back where it belongs. I shift my weight, hear the squish, feel the icky cold dampness.

"I'm fine," I mumble. "It makes me nervous, people touching me."

"That's like this kid in my calculus class. He sits in a corner because he doesn't want anyone near him, but he's pure genius. He says he has some form of autism."

I smile. Antonio understands. Like Mrs. Mac. "Asperger's syndrome," I tell him. "It comes from a genetic mutation. My father had cancer before I was born, and I think . . ."

Antonio holds his hand out, palm up, as if telling me to stop.

"Max must have told you," I say.

"No. He never said anything." Antonio bites his lower lip, and I wonder how good a friend Max was if Antonio didn't know a basic fact about our family. "My father had cancer too," he says softly. "But he . . . didn't . . . make it."

"He died?"

Antonio nods.

"Is that why you have the Livestrong tattoo?" Today the shirt covers it up, but I know it's there, and it'll be there forever.

"Yeah."

"Even though Lance Armstrong didn't die either?"

Antonio grimaces, and I realize I said the wrong thing. But he doesn't call me stupid or retard or freak, like most kids would. Instead, he reaches into a cargo pocket, pulls out his wallet, and slides a photo from behind what looks like his driver's license. I notice UNDER 21 in big red letters on the license.

He hands me the photo. The way Mr. Elliott and Dad traded photos with each other this morning. "My father."

The man has deep-set eyes, a narrow face, and straight, dark hair. Antonio's hair is lighter and wavy, and his face fuller. I think this man in the picture already looks sick, with sunken cheeks and thin lips.

"I'm sorry," I mumble. I know it's what I'm supposed to say when I hear that someone has died, even though it isn't my fault that he died.

I give the photo back to Antonio. He slides it into his wallet.

Antonio and I never get to the BMX track that day. Instead, he shows me the entire route of trails, though many of them are too hard for me to ride and I have to walk my bike across them or go around them. Standing on the opposite bank, I record him riding the narrow single track that he tells me Ice Age glaciers carved into the rock above the creek. At one point he drops six feet from a rock to a root-rutted dirt path and crosses the creek atop a fallen tree trunk.

"How do you do that?" I ask him while I play back my recording. He stands beside me and peers over my shoulder at the tiny image of his daredevil ride.

"It's all balance. Speed. How you use gravity." He strips off his gloves and holds them in one hand. I turn to face him.

"But the tree? It's not flat on top. Did you ever fall off one and end up in the water?"

Antonio nods. "Lots of times. You can't slow down. If you get scared and slow down . . ." He makes a chopping motion with his free hand. Like sliding into the water.

"Ouch," I say.

"Yeah." He points to a scar that starts at the bottom of his cargo shorts and runs about six inches down his calf. "Got that one in a race a year ago. Thirty-five stitches. Still finished the race, though."

I play the video again, looking for any wobble on the tree, anyplace Antonio slowed down. I don't find any.

From behind me comes Antonio's voice. "My dad taught me everything about riding." He pauses. "My bike . . . it used to be his."

I squeeze the battered red bike's front tire, rock-hard and slick from riding through mud. "I can put music with the videos," I say, because I already told him I was sorry about his father. "Anything you like?"

"You heard of Rage Against the Machine? They're my favorite band."

"Max likes them too." Even though they're totally different from our family's band.

"I know," Antonio says.

I stare at his hands, at the rope bracelet on his left wrist and the gloves in his right hand. I don't want to be afraid of touching him. He's Max's friend, which almost makes him my big brother too.

I hold my hand out toward Antonio and close my eyes. My fingers close over the stiff, scratchy bracelet. I let my hand slip down until it reaches his calloused palm. He squeezes. A current runs through me. *Wolverine's special powers?* I open my eyes.

Antonio is smiling.

# CHAPTER 16

INSTEAD OF FINISHING MY HOMEWORK FOR MS. LATIMER, I make the video of Antonio's ride. The music is as chaotic as a tangle of roots, as angry as knobby tires tearing up packed dirt. I pound my fist on my desk in time to the beat. I can't concentrate on anything except the images of Wolverine, Antonio, his red bike that once belonged to his father, the twisting trails, and Rage Against the Machine.

That's what music does for me. It shows me the emotion that Mr. Internet says we Asperger's mutants have trouble understanding. When I hear the songs, I get that Antonio beats up his bike and his body on the trail because he's angry at what happened to his father. I also understand that he misses his father the way I miss Mami, but while Mami can come back anytime she wants, his father will never come back.

I call the video "Riding the Rock" and sign up for a new name on YouTube because I can't use Corazondeleste when the band doesn't exist. "Rogue" comes to me right away, but someone else already took it, so I have to add numbers. I pick 266, the numbers on the license plate of Dad's pickup. When I turn sixteen, I'll get to drive it.

In the morning I upload the video and wait for the views. Ten in the first hour. Nearly 100 when Ms. Latimer shows up. After she leaves, 259. An hour later when I'm packing the video camera to ride to College Park, 318.

As I ride, I recite the numbers in my head. They make me feel powerful. Instead of bad things happening to me—Mami leaving, my brother Eli saying I shouldn't have been born, Mr. Mac dying and Mrs. Mac moving away, New Kids dumping me, Chad using me for his parents' meth cooking—I'm the one in charge. I have some kind of special power, even if I don't know exactly what it is yet.

I find Antonio and three other boys in the field next to the BMX pit, digging holes in the grass with a shovel. Antonio lets his shovel drop and trots over to me. When I dismount, my legs get tangled in the bike. Antonio steadies me by holding my elbow, but I stiffen and fall anyway.

I untangle my foot and brush myself off, hoping none of the other boys noticed my clumsy entrance. "Guys, this is Max's little sister. Kiara," Antonio calls out.

"No way." I recognize the kid with the sideburns from my trip with Chad on Saturday. "You're, like, big."

Antonio introduces them to me. The one with the sideburns, who had the video camera, is called Veg. Then there's Kevin, nicknamed Cap'n Crunch—he's tall and blond, and I also saw him on Saturday. The one I never saw before is Brian, known as Dunk. He wears a helmet even though he's not riding but digging. I repeat their names and nick-names in my mind, but I know I won't remember them. I never do.

"She's going to help record our stunts." Antonio turns to me. "Unless you want to ride, that is."

"Nah." I'd probably fall on the first mound and hurt my-self. Lowering my voice so only Antonio can hear me, I add, "I'll stay behind the scenes. Invisible." The way I'm used to being. The way I was when I came here with Chad.

"Like water."

"Like water?" I shake my head, confused.

"Yeah. Water goes where it wants to go. Breaks through everything in its way." I peek above the screen at Antonio. The other boys talk about their bikes, their tricks, impress-ing the girls from College Park High School who they say show up to watch them sometimes. Antonio says unexpected things, as if beneath the mountain biker surface—the hel-met, the tattoo, the talk about "sick trails"—a different person lives. A moody Wolverine with a tragic past.

I stand next to Antonio while he works. He tells me they're clearing a single-track trail next to the BMX track and building a ladder bridge with logs from the tree that fell down two weeks ago, the one he was cutting with the chain saw when Chad and I met him. My face flushes when I think of him catching us with those four nasty bottles.

"I uploaded the video of you this morning," I tell him, to chase that first meeting from my mind.

"I'll have to check it out. How many hits so far?"

"Three hundred eighteen. I checked before I left."

A grin breaks out across Antonio's face. "That's way better than Veg's average. And it's only been what . . . five hours?"

"Six."

"He doesn't hold the camera still. That's why he doesn't get any hits." Antonio pushes his hand through his hair. "Your school lets you put videos on YouTube?"

I swallow, choke. "I was . . . kicked out of school."

"What?"

I tell him about Melanie Prince-Parker and the lunch tray. Not even Max knows about this, but I tell Antonio as if he's the only person in the world who'd understand. Who might even be proud of me for standing up to the mean girls. My throat and chest relax as I speak. My words trip over each other.

"That's heavy duty," he says when I finish. He steps backward, and the tight band snaps around my lungs again. Maybe he wasn't so impressed after all. "Now I see why you thought you'd end up in juvie."

"Yeah." I stare at the churned-up dirt and grass. "I guess you think I'm pretty weird."

If he were Wolverine and I were Rogue, he'd invite me to join the X-Men now. He'd lure me away from Mystique's Brotherhood of Evil Mutants by showing me how to use my special powers to help the world instead of destroying things and avenging those who mistreated me.

When Chad tutored me, he told me not to talk about the X-Men, so I press my lips together and wait for Antonio to say something.

He doesn't get the chance.

A scream from the top of the hill is followed by a whooshing sound. I spin around to see Chad riding down the hill at full speed toward the BMX track. But this time his wheel skims a rock, he wobbles slightly, and when he hits the mound, he goes airborne at an angle. After a single 360 he lands on his front tire near the bottom of the mound and flies headfirst over the handlebars. The bike skids in one direction, Chad on his stomach on the other.

"Oof!" Veg calls out.

Antonio glares at me. "I told that little dirtbag not to come here."

"I didn't bring him." I feel the burn of Antonio's eyes. "Well, I did, but . . ." *But he wanted to hang out with your friends and they didn't talk to me, so I went home.* I try to tell him that, but the words don't come out. And Chad lies on the ground, motionless.

I run to Chad, stumble in the sand, dust myself off. Lying facedown, he gasps for breath.

"I . . . can't . . . move," he says.

I stop a few feet away, afraid to come closer.

*Please be all right. Please be all right.*

Chad pops to his hands and knees, T-shirted back heaving. I notice Antonio and the guy with the helmet standing next to him. "Wind . . . knocked . . . out . . . of me." Chad flops onto his stomach again.

I take a deep breath. "That's all? Like a plopped-on whoopee cushion."

He coughs. "Not . . . funny."

"You know what's not funny?" says a deep voice behind me. "Me missing this shot."

I turn around to see Veg's face over my shoulder. "Sorry. Missed the shot too," I say, tugging the strap of my backpack, feeling the weight of my camcorder inside. "At least he's okay."

"We could have had a thousand hits," Veg says. He holds up his camera. "What would we call it?"

"Raggedy Chad," I answer. He looked like a scrawny rag doll when he skidded belly-down in the dirt. Everyone laughs but Antonio.

Chad climbs to his feet, swaying a little. "That was sick! I wanna go again!" he says.

Antonio grabs his arm. "Kid, what did I tell you about not coming here?"

"Don't hurt him." My words come out as a squeak.

Chad shouts past me, spit flying, "I don't have anything."

"Dude, he's cool. You should see him ride," Kevin says.

And I could record Chad. Make videos with different kinds of music for the sound track. Get thousands of hits for rogue266. I wouldn't have just one friend or two friends, but all the kids at the BMX track as my friends— like finally getting to sit at the popular girls' table. My lip trembles. "Come on, Antonio. Let him stay," I say, my voice so weak that I'm not sure Antonio hears me.

Before I can open my mouth to say it again, Antonio bends down to Chad's level and peers into his face. "Get a helmet," he says. "We can't have any injuries here, or we'll be in a pile of trouble."

I wave my hand. "You can use mine. I cleaned it."

The kid with the helmet, whose name I forgot, knocks the top of his. "I'll let you borrow this one. But I want her to record me first."

"Cool." Chad turns his gaze from the other kid to me. "Nothing against you, Kiara. But he has a real skater helmet with stickers."

"Lemme see your camera." Veg stands next to me. I hand him mine and he compares it to his, in his other hand. Mine is smaller, but it has more buttons. "You got a really nice one," he says. "You can zoom in a lot closer and adjust for light."

"I know," I answer. "I used it to make videos of my family's band."

"Great," Veg says. "Now that you're here, I'm gonna ride."

"Helmets, everybody, remember," Antonio cuts in. Stepping closer to me, he adds, "Veg had a really bad concussion last year."

"Which is how I got my name. My real name's Steve."

A long whistle interrupts us. I cover my ears. Helmet kid takes his fingers from his mouth and shouts, "We're wasting daylight here, camerapeople."

"Yeah. And I'm next after he's done." Chad jumps up and down.

"Better get to work," Antonio says. "These BMX guys like to fight over who gets camera time. Now that you're getting hits, it's going to be a lot worse."

Veg hands back my camera, and I apologize to the kid who was waiting. When I press the button, he leans into the camera, says simply, "Brian Gerardi," and rides off. My recording catches Chad's breathy voice describing the kid's perfect tailwhip.

Their arguments about whose turn it is make me think of that awful birthday party where the girls said I cut in line when I didn't. But somehow the boys work it all out. As I record them, I imagine them as my X-Men. With his wild hair and sideburns and sense of humor, Veg reminds me of Beast. Kevin, the tall, pale one, is Iceman. Brian, who doesn't talk much, is Colossus because Colossus doesn't talk much either.

All week long, I tell myself, *I have friends.* The bike trails are my popular girls' table, even though everyone there but me is a boy.

# CHAPTER 17

*A FEW NEW KIDS SHOW UP ON SATURDAY, AND EVEN THOUGH* they pay more attention to Chad, they talk to me too. They ask me things like, *Did you get that amazing stunt?* and *How many hits do you have?* and *Will you make a video of me?* I organize the line and make sure everyone gets a turn.

"What do I have now?" Antonio asks me.

I flip to the page in my notebook where I've kept count from Monday to this morning. "'Riding the Rock'—one thousand, one hundred twenty-four." I pause. "'Crash Splash'"—Wednesday's wipeout caused by a homemade bridge with an unexpectedly missing board—"one thousand, five hundred thirty-six."

Brian stands in front of me. I move my finger to his line. "'Perfect Ten Tailwhip'—five-oh-five. Sorry." He nods and steps back.

"Me! Me! Me!" Chad twirls in front of me.

I'm especially proud of "Gambit Double 360," with his stunt in slow motion to Nirvana's "Smells Like Teen Spirit."

"You have one thousand, three hundred eleven hits. In just two days."

Chad stops abruptly and blows his breath through pursed lips. "You mean I didn't beat him." He points to Antonio.

"His went up a day ahead of yours. You might catch up," I say.

But Veg calls out from behind Chad, "Nah. People like the wipeouts best."

All the way home, Chad begs me to make a new video of him. So even though his father is an evil creep who I never want to see again, I go to the park on Sunday morning to record him and Dad playing bluegrass together. This time Brandon comes outside with his father, and I'm glad because I can pay attention to Brandon and not look at his dad. Or mine.

Except that my dad decides to start up a conversation. "You're even cuter than your picture," he tells Brandon.

Brandon grins. Dad musses his hair.

Brandon puts both his hands on his hips. "My daddy says you were in a band." I think he's more impressed about the band than Chad ever was.

"Sure was." Dad starts to tell Brandon about Corazón del Este, but banjo music drowns him out, Mr. Elliott telling Dad without words to quit the chitchat and play. Brandon sits on the platform next to Dad and kicks his little feet in time to the music. I stare at those feet while I hold my microphone in front of the guitar and the banjo.

I use one of the tunes as the sound track of a new video I

title "Hanging Chad." In it Chad hangs weightless in the air for what seems like forever, his bike dangling from one hand.

At three in the afternoon I hit the upload button and wait for the views. I think it's my best video ever, even better than "Gambit Double 360" because the stunt is so graceful and the music captures Chad's hyper energy so perfectly. I have a hundred views in the first hour. Maybe this video will give Chad the most attention since he wants it so badly.

Mami calls at seven that night. After Dad talks with her, going upstairs to do it in private, he hands his cell phone to me. He's smiling, as if he thinks there's good news on the other end.

*Is Mami coming home after all?*

The phone is greasy from hands that have been sautéing vegetables for ratatouille, Dad trying for more variety with the dinner menu. I think I maybe had something to do with it. After my meltdown over the takeout pizza, I made a list of cheap and easy dinner ideas, asked Mr. Internet for the recipes, and gave them to Dad. I'm happy that he's cooking, but he makes a big mess that I have to clean up. I wipe the back of the phone on my jeans and the screen and keypad with my shirttail. Good news can wait until Dad's phone isn't disgusting anymore.

"*Hola, Mami. Te extraño.*"

"I miss you too," she says in Spanish. Her English isn't very good because she was already sixteen when she fled to Canada with her mother and her two younger brothers, my *tíos* Mauricio and Rogelio, after their father was killed back in El Salvador. And in Montreal, they speak mainly French.

Mami said you have to start speaking another language when you're a baby or you'll always speak it with an accent. When I stopped talking in kindergarten, my *abuela* in Montreal said it was because I got confused with parents who taught me two languages at the same time when I was a baby. But I know that's not the real reason. You don't become a mutant by learning too many languages at once but by messed-up DNA.

My mouth is dry when I speak again. "I want you to come home."

*Quiero que vuelvas a casa* . . . The subjunctive. That's what I like about Spanish. It has rules to tell you about emotion. *I want. I wish. I need. I hope. I dream. I'm sorry.* When you know something's sure to happen, you don't use the subjunctive. You use the indicative. When something might not happen, or has no chance at all of happening, or you really, really want it to happen, that's the subjunctive. In Spanish you know the difference. English doesn't use the subjunctive nearly as much, so a person can lie, and the words don't tell you he's lying. They don't tell you what a person is feeling, and without the right words to tell me, I don't understand.

"That's what I called about," Mami says.

"Yay!" I shout in English, then switch back to Spanish. "When are you coming?"

The phone line crackles. Some cell tower or satellite

between northeastern Connecticut and Montreal must have burped. *Come on,* I mouth.

"We've decided you're spending the summer here."

"What?"

She repeats the words. *Hemos decidido que pasarás el verano aquí* . . . The indicative.

"NO!" I yell. Dad slips through the open doorway from the kitchen into the living room. Making his escape rather than helping me. Abandoning dinner preparations too.

"I thought that's what you wanted," she says.

"Where did you get that idea?"

"You were telling your father." She pauses. I hear Dad's footsteps going up the stairs. "How much you missed me."

Right. In Dad's truck. The day I met Antonio and found out about the bottles Chad made me carry. Stupid me.

I whack my head with the edge of Dad's phone.

"I didn't want to leave here. I wanted you to come back."

"Kiara, *amor* . . ."

*Amor?* Like she really loves me? Or is she just saying that to get me to do what she wants?

Mami continues. "It works out best this way. I can see you. And your father wants to play festivals this summer."

"So it's all about him! And his stupid festivals!" I stomp my foot. The house vibrates.

"What's going on, Kiara?" I hear Dad's voice from upstairs and stalk toward the stairs.

"Liar! You said you'd bring me to the festivals. And now you're shipping me away," I yell up to Dad. Even if I miss some weekends, I'll still be able to see my friends if I stay with Dad. If I go to Montreal, it's all over.

Mami's voice sounds tinny. "Max will be here. They liked his audition and hired him to play keyboards."

"I don't care!" I don't tell her that my new friend Antonio is even nicer than Max. He doesn't talk about me being different—or hard to handle.

"At the end of the summer, we can all come back together."

"First you said you'd be home in May. Now you're saying the end of the summer." I rub my eyes with the back of my hand. When people lie to me once, I never can believe them again. "How do I know you won't decide to stay there forever?"

The moment of silence tells me she doesn't have an answer. "After school's out—"

"No!" Another stomp. "No. No. No. No. No."

Does she even know I'm not in school anymore? I don't plan to tell her because then she won't do anything I want her to do.

"Your father will drive you up," she continues as soon as I stop saying my noes to take a breath.

"He wants you to come home too, Mami. He wants you and him to be together." She hasn't heard his songs in minor keys. If she did, she'd cry and realize he can't live without her.

And I can't leave my friends. *I can't.*

I think of Chad, launching himself into the air with his bicycle, twisting and spinning against the laws of gravity. My mind flashes to Brandon with his wrestlers, how we keep each other company in the park in the time between when Ms. Latimer leaves and when the middle-school bus arrives.

I can't forget the rest of the guys either, my own X-Men—Veg, Kevin, and Brian. Beast, Iceman, and Colossus.

Above me, the floorboards groan. It's all up to me to bring Mami back.

"I have friends here, Mami. *Friends.*"

"Yes. Your father mentioned a new boy."

"You don't get it. If I go, they'll forget all about me. They'll make other friends and I'll be alone again. Is that what you want?" My voice rises an octave. "Is that what you want? No friends?"

"Kiara, *listen.*"

"Don't . . . make . . . me . . . leave . . . my . . . friends. Please!" The phone slides down my face. I push it back up. "Please."

"I'm sure they'll be there when you get back."

"No, they won't!"

Mami clears her throat. "I haven't seen you since—"

"And whose decision was that?"

"Don't interrupt, or there will be consequences."

*Like what? You'll spank me and put me in time-out, from three hundred miles away?* That's what she used to do when I was younger. She never hit me hard, but what really stung was my brothers watching bad little Kiara get her punishment.

"You won't be bored. I promise," Mami says. "You can

work on your French. And if your father doesn't mind you bringing the camcorder, you can record us."

"I'm doing it here. That new kid? He does cool bike stunts. You should see my videos." I stop to take a quick breath. "And he's helping me. He's my . . . tutor. And way cooler, because he's my age and you aren't."

She sighs. "Are you done?"

I can't think of anything more to say that'll change her mind. And maybe I shouldn't have said Chad was way cooler and she's old, but it's the truth. "I guess." I squeeze the phone, as if I could choke off her words.

"He's not going anywhere."

"No!" I can't stop my tears now. "He'll find some other friend he likes better. Like all the rest of them."

"Don't argue. It's final. As soon as school's out, get your things ready." The imperative has the same verb form as the subjunctive when it's a "no." And after that, it doesn't matter. I don't have a choice. I'm a little girl who can be dragged from one place to another without anyone caring what she wants. Inside my head, I'm screaming, and it drowns out most of what she says about Dad and my *abuela* and touring with her new band.

"I hate you! I never want to see you again!" Blindly, I slam the flip phone shut and hurl it across the kitchen. It hits the door frame and splits apart, one half skittering behind the refrigerator and the other bouncing toward me.

# CHAPTER 18

FOR SMASHING DAD'S CELL PHONE, I GET MY COMPUTER
taken away. Dad carries it piece by piece to the living room
and sets it up again on a table he brought up from the basement. From now until the end of school, he'll let me use it to
do my homework, but when he's not watching me, he locks
away the power cord.

I might as well forget I had a computer. After the end of
school I'm leaving for Montreal, so I'll never get to use it for
what I want anyway.

I don't ride to College Park the next day because I don't
know how to tell Antonio and the other guys that my video
career is finished. Chad rides away as soon as the middle-
school bus drops him off, but he comes home two hours
later and stays in the park until late at night. I suspect
that his parents are cooking again. I don't tell him what
happened either.

Three straight days of rain, from Tuesday through
Thursday, postpone the moment when I have to tell the

truth. I repeat in my mind the words I can't bear to say aloud. *I had a mega-meltdown. I've been punished, but it's your punishment too because you don't get your videos made and uploaded.* I hate it when everyone gets punished because one person messed up. And once they find out I'm the person who messed up, they won't want to be my friend.

So even though I wake up to sunshine on Friday morning, I decide not to go to the bike track. I'd rather just disappear than say what happened and watch them dump me.

Ms. Latimer notices that I'm paying a lot more attention to my schoolwork. "Right in time. You have two weeks until the exams," she says on Friday. I stare at the useless hulk of my computer in the corner of the room.

"So what happens if someone doesn't pass?" Like Chad. I don't think he has a chance. I only got to tutor him once and he didn't listen to me then.

"Summer school, then a retest. I don't think that's an issue with you." Ms. Latimer smiles. "You'll make me proud. And in the fall, you'll start high school as if none of this trouble ever happened."

My chest tightens at the mention of high school. Where I'll be back in class with the mean kids. Or in the ED/LD class, which means Emotionally Disturbed/Learning Disabled. Kind of like the place where Temple Grandin's parents sent her, except not a boarding school. I don't know whether the regular class or the special class is worse. "Are they going to put me with the special kids?"

Ms. Latimer clears her throat. "Look at me, Kiara." I

force my eyes away from the dead computer and toward her face. One time, she told me I should leave every conversation knowing what color the other person's eyes are. Hers are green. Around her neck, a silver cross hangs from a shiny chain. "You've worked hard, and you deserve a fresh start. I'm recommending you see a counselor once a week for anger management but attend regular classes." She pauses. "Honors classes, of course."

I gaze at my hands, at my bitten-off fingernails. I don't think Dad told her about my latest tantrum and my punishment. She hasn't asked why my computer suddenly appeared in the living room.

I can't go away all summer, or my friends will forget me. Veg will make the videos again, which means he won't get to ride and no one will want to watch us.

That's right. *Us.* I belong to this group. I'm the invisible one behind the screen.

I saw Veg's videos. Antonio's right. He doesn't hold the camera steady, so the track bounces up and down along with the riders. He doesn't put any music in the background either. You have to use the right music to make people feel how scary and thrilling it is to fly through the air or crash to the ground and flop like a rag doll.

People really do like the wipeouts best. The one of Antonio falling off the bridge into the creek, which I put with the music of Rage Against the Machine, was still leading in hits the night I crashed and flopped by not convincing Mami to let me stay. I have no idea how "Hanging Chad" is doing. If he asks me, I have nothing to tell him.

Rogue wouldn't let Mystique and the Brotherhood of Evil Mutants snatch her back once she'd joined the X-Men. Maybe my X-Men can come up with a way to keep me from having to leave. But that means I have to tell them the truth first—and hope they'll be on my side.

# CHAPTER 19

*AFTER MS. LATIMER DRIVES OFF, I GO TO THE BACKYARD AND*
pretend I'm playing in the cypress trees next to the bayou
where Rogue used to play before her mother left. Now that
it's the middle of May, the oak tree's leaves have finally
burst from their buds, making a canopy of green that nearly
blocks out the sun. Like the trees of Cajun country. Like the
posters on my bedroom wall.

I hear the afternoon bus's squealing brakes, and a little
later Brandon comes out of his house with his box of wrestlers. "Have you seen my brother?" he asks.

"No. Is his bike there?"

Brandon crosses the street, peers into the garage, then
disappears from my view. I guess he's checking inside the
garage, blocked by his family's van in the driveway.

He skips across the street to the park, where I wait for
him. "No bike. But his school stuff is there."

"He must have gone riding. Ever seen his tricks?"

"Yeah. They're the best." Brandon flashes his missing-teeth smile. "He says he's gonna teach me when I'm bigger."

Brandon and I play wrestlers in the park. From time to time he glances toward Washington Avenue, and around five thirty, women's voices from his backyard interrupt our tag team match. I don't see anyone because the garage is in the way. A green station wagon is parked on the street in front of the house. The quieter voice sounds scratchy like Mrs. Mac's, but I miss many of the words. The other person's words I make out.

*We have a lease, hear? A lease. Take us to court for this mess—which we're cleaning up—and we'll take you to court for the car accident. Say you were drunk and paid us to cover it up . . .*

I squeeze the wrestler tight, as if The Rock could keep me from running across the street to defend Mrs. Mac. She wasn't drunk that night. She gave me a book and tried to help me.

*You have no right to sell the house right out from under us.*

Mrs. Mac is selling her house?

Chad rounds the corner on his BMX bike and rides toward us with his front wheel spinning in the air, at the level of his face. He wears no helmet. Antonio gave him an old helmet, but he always leaves it at the track, underneath a jump where several of the kids leave theirs.

His brakes squeal. "Wassup, Bran-my-man?" He holds out his palm for Brandon to slap. When Brandon slaps it, Chad laughs and says, "Harder. Put some muscle into it."

Brandon winds his arm behind him and slams his little palm against Chad's.

Chad laughs again. "There you go." He musses his little brother's hair. Then he cocks his head toward the voices. "What's going on?"

Brandon shrugs.

"I'm here. You can go in now," Chad tells him. But Brandon shakes his head. When Chad speaks again, his voice is low and shaky. "No one messed with you?"

"Nuh-uh," Brandon mumbles. "But there were too many bags, so—"

Chad cuts him off. "I'll take care of it."

He pushes his bike across the street. A skinny woman who must be Mrs. Elliott pops out from behind the garage. "Where the hell have you been?" she screams. "That old lady's gonna kick us out because of the mess you left!"

Brandon's lip trembles, and he lowers his eyes to his tag team battle. He makes the Miz action figure pound in Kristal's head while John Cena jumps on her feet, pushing them deeper into the mud.

I glance back to the scene across the street. Chad's mother grabs a handful of his T-shirt and drags him inside. I don't see Mrs. Mac.

"Chad gonna get a whuppin'," Brandon says softly.

"Because of . . . the bags?" *What bags,* I wonder. *Could they be moving again? Is Mrs. Mac kicking them out?*

"'Cause he's late. He's always late."

"He should get to ride his bike." It's the only good thing in his life. He said it himself. He'd even risk a *whuppin'* to ride.

Which is more than I'd do for my videos. Or to stay here with my friends this summer.

I hear someone call my name. It's not Brandon, with his click-clack of wrestlers hitting each other and occasional "Bam" and "Pow" under his breath.

I twist around. Mrs. Mac sits on the concrete platform at the other end of the park. She lifts her head from her hands and says, "Come here, Kiara."

I tell Brandon to stay where he is, and I go to her. I take a seat on the bench a few feet away, pull my knees to my chest, and wrap my arms around my legs. "What is it, Mrs. Mac?" I ask. I wonder if she's upset because of the way Mrs. Elliott yelled at her.

Mrs. Mac lets out a long sigh. "I wanted to let you know. I'm moving to Philadelphia next week." She tells me she's going to live in what's called shared housing, but it sounds like a commune of old people. They grow their own food, cook and eat together, don't drive, and live in a way that sustains the environment. It sounds kind of cool, like someplace I'd want to live if I got old and turned into a bad driver. "Will you tell your dad?" she says.

I check my wristwatch. "He'll be home in less than an hour."

"My sister needs her car back. And . . ." Mrs. Mac clears her throat. "Your dad and I aren't on the best of terms right now."

I think of my dismantled computer. "Yeah, he and I aren't either." I run my fingernail along the cement platform. "What did you do?"

"Be a buttinsky." She winks at me.

"What's a buttinsky?" I repeat the word in my mind because it sounds so funny. *Butt-in-skee.*

"Someone who meddles in other people's business. People don't seem to like it much."

Suddenly I feel hot all over, my mouth so parched I can't swallow. I guess Dad didn't like her telling him that I have the same thing that Temple Grandin does. He still thinks I'm just immature and miss my mother and can't control my temper.

I don't want Mrs. Mac to feel like it's her fault when she tried to help me, so I say, "Dad's been having problems. Because of Mami leaving."

"I know." Mrs. Mac pats my knee. I twist away.

"I told her she should come back." A loose strand of hair tickles my nose. I try to blow it to the side. "But she and Dad are making me go to Montreal for the summer."

"You should spend time with your mother." Mrs. Mac pushes the hair from my face. "Yasmín misses you."

"No, she doesn't. She left without me." My mind returns to my brothers' conversation. "Maybe she got tired of me acting up all the time."

"That's not the reason. Her job was only supposed to be for a few months."

I cut in. "Which turned into another few months."

"And you were still in school."

"I'm not in school now." *But Mami doesn't know that!* Dad didn't tell her because if he did, she'd really hate me.

I swallow, and it feels like bits of glass in my throat.

"You still have the tutor, don't you?"

My gaze drops to my sneakers. "For two more weeks. I don't want to go."

"Your mother wants to see you. She said when I talked to her—"

"When did you talk to her?" Does Mami know everything, thanks to Mrs. Mac's being a *buttinsky*?

"Oh, I don't remember, dear. Sometime before the accident." Mrs. Mac reaches out her hand, and this time I scoot back before she can touch me. I don't like her taking Mami's side.

"Why were you and Mrs. Elliott arguing?" I ask to change the subject.

"Have you seen my backyard?"

"Not in a while." I remember the honeysuckle that Mrs. Mac used to grow there, its sweet smell, and how she used to wear its flowers in her hair. Once when my parents went away for a concert tour, she made me a crown of honeysuckle and let me put on one of her dresses, and she and Mr. Mac called me their nature princess. After Mr. Mac died, the bushes turned brown, and so did the rest of their garden. Then she moved out and Chad's family moved in.

"You should see it." Mrs. Mac points toward her house. The one she's leaving forever and maybe even selling. "I asked her to clean it up. That's when she started screaming at me."

"It's not you. She's mean to everyone." I press my lips together. Just like I can't tell Dad, I can't snitch about the drugs to Mrs. Mac because she's a *buttinsky,* and the

Elliotts and the people they work for may even track her all the way to Philadelphia, where a bunch of old hippies would be no match for a drug gang.

"I'm going to miss you, dear Kiara."

I blink a few times. Dirt in my eye. "I'm going to miss you too."

"Things have been hard for both of us," Mrs. Mac says. "I wish there was more I could have done."

"You gave me that book. About the lady like me who has a talent for understanding animals." I survey the park, the sun setting pink and purple overhead, Brandon playing in the pile of dirt in the opposite corner where the sandbox used to be. A squirrel skitters across a branch of the oak tree and stops above us. I stare at his fluffy white underbelly and his tiny paws touching his nose, as if he's praying.

Mrs. Mac holds her arms outstretched. When I don't move, she says, "Can I get a good-bye hug, dear?"

"Sure." Slowly, I embrace her.

"Sometimes it takes time to find your place," Mrs. Mac says, not letting me go. "But you're a special person, and I know you'll do great things."

"Special?" Like the special classes they may put me in? Or the special powers that the X-Men have?

I rest my head on Mrs. Mac's shoulder, feel her damp crinkly blouse against my eyelids. "Special is good," she says. "You may not understand it now, but one day you will. And then"—she lowers her arms and kisses the top of my head—"the world will be a better place because of you."

"Like that lady in the book?" I can't tell her I haven't

read a word since the day I first met Brandon in the park. The torn dust jacket still marks the place in chapter three where I quit.

"Yes. Like Temple Grandin. But whatever you do, it will be something all your own."

Now I have to finish the book to find out what she did so I don't try to do the same thing.

I give Mrs. Mac a weak wave as she walks toward her borrowed car, filled with the last of her boxes. Her words echo: The world will be a better place because of *me*?

I figure out the equation in my mind.

In one column: Five music videos with over a thousand hits total. Five bike videos with nearly five thousand hits total. I guess if people watched, the videos made them happy.

In the other column: One knocked-out tooth. At least it was a baby tooth. One ruined birthday cake. A lot of pulled-out hair. One bloody nose and sweater. One busted friendship between a buttinsky and a dad who won't face the truth.

One worn-out and angry mother.

One broken family.

# CHAPTER 20

*I WAKE UP EARLY THE NEXT MORNING AND CAN'T GET BACK* to sleep. I think of Mrs. Mac leaving and what she said about me doing great things and the world being a better place because of me. If so, I need to start putting more things in my good column.

But what?

Around nine, I hear the Elliotts' van coughing to life and driving away. The sounds of the Elliotts leaving give me an idea. Now that they're gone, I can sneak into the backyard and clean it up. Then Mrs. Mac's yard won't be a mess, and Chad and Brandon won't get in any more trouble with their mom.

Saturday is Dad's day off—his one day to sleep in—and I slip downstairs without waking him. Remembering the bottle of muriatic acid I found under the porch steps, I grab a pair of work gloves, a bandanna, and an armful of black garbage bags from the basement.

I squeeze through the hole in the fence and cross the

park. As soon as I step onto the curb on the Elliotts' side of Cherry Street, I hear rustling. And Chad's and Brandon's voices.

I press myself against the house, where they can't see me. I thought the whole family had left together, but I was wrong.

Chad's voice drifts toward me. "Get under the back stairs where you stuffed the trash bags. Mom and Dad said we better have this cleaned up by the time they get back, or else . . ."

So their parents left them alone? And they don't have much time to clean up whatever mess Mrs. Mac saw.

I've tied the bandanna around my neck to keep from inhaling any chemical fumes, and now I tug it over my mouth and nose. Several garbage bags slide from my grasp. I leave them at the corner of the house and creep forward.

When I see their yard, I gasp. I wasn't prepared for so much trash—everywhere are sooty two-liter soda bottles like the ones Antonio caught us with, bottles of Drano, and piles of random garbage.

And most of Mrs. Mac's garden is dead.

The two boys, their blond hair shiny in the morning sunlight, stand next to the rusted metal stairs to the basement. Brandon gets onto his hands and knees beside the stairs, where there's a space large enough for a cat to crawl into, but not a boy in kindergarten. He sticks both arms in, then his head, and tries to wriggle his shoulders inside.

*He's going to get stuck,* I think.

But he doesn't. After a while, he inches himself out of the hole, holding a roll of empty bags. Dirt streaks his face and covers his hair and skinny arms.

*He didn't have to do that. I brought bags.* But it's too late.

Chad carries a bag to a toxic pile and starts filling it. "So you didn't clean up any of this yesterday when Mom told you to?" he asks Brandon.

"I was waiting for you." No wonder Brandon kept asking me if I knew where his brother had gone. Brandon continues. "I started, but it was too hard. I hid the rest of the bags under the stairs till you got back."

I remember Brandon telling me why Chad got in trouble with his mother: *'Cause he's late. He's always late.* And I told Brandon that Chad should be able to ride his bike.

Still, there's no way Brandon could have cleaned up this whole mess by himself.

And who dumped this garbage in the yard in the first place? Not Chad and Brandon, but parents who didn't care about them or Mrs. Mac's yard.

I can't let Chad and Brandon do this all by themselves and with nothing to protect them from the chemicals. I step into the yard. Chad and Brandon face the other direction and my feet don't make any noise on the damp ground, so they don't notice me at first.

Then Brandon calls out, "Hey, look, there's Kiara!" He runs toward me and wraps his grubby hands around my legs. "You look like a cowboy!"

"You shouldn't be cleaning up this stuff without gloves."

I take off my gloves and wave them above Brandon's head.

"Can't hear you," Brandon says, and I realize I didn't remove the bandanna covering my mouth.

I drop the gloves, untie the blue cloth with its white curlicue pattern, and tie it around Brandon's neck. "There. Now you're the cowboy." I pat his dust-caked hair.

"Yay! I'm a cowboy!" Brandon runs to his brother and pretends to shoot him, both thumbs up and index fingers outstretched. "Bang, bang, you're dead."

*Bang. You dead.* I wait for Gambit to respond with his famous line. Instead, Chad lifts the bag to his shoulder like a skinny blond Santa Claus. "Get out of here, Kiara. This is none of your business," he says. I wonder what kind of trouble he got into for riding his bike at the BMX track rather than helping Brandon with the nasty garbage.

I inch backward. "I can bring you gloves too, Chad. And help you guys clean up."

"We don't need you," Chad says. "Go."

*Why don't you care about getting poisoned?* Before I leave, I pick my gloves off the ground and slide them over Brandon's little hands. Then I pull up the bandanna to cover his nose and mouth. His hands and face are dirty but soft and unmarred—not hard like his brother's. Chad snorts and goes back to picking up trash bare-handed, the black bag dragging across the dirt and weeds.

I started out the morning ready to put more things in my good column. But Chad doesn't want me here.

Maybe I should only do things that I want to do. Forget about making the world a better place, at least for now. I want to make videos at the bike track and stay in town with all the new friends I've made.

On the way back to my house, I decide three more things. One: If Chad can take a huge risk to do the thing he most wants to do, so can I. Two: I don't have to tell Antonio the truth about why my computer got taken away. I can tell him I spent too much time on the videos and quit doing my homework. That's a much cooler reason for getting into trouble than what I really did. And three: I don't have to tell Dad the truth about anything.

I write Dad a note that I'm going to the town library to work on an assignment for Ms. Latimer—thanks to him not being awake to give me the power cord for my computer. Then I collect my backpack with Dad's camera, roll Max's bike out from under the lean-to, and for the first time all week ride to my friends in College Park.

# CHAPTER 21

*I TAKE THE END-OF-YEAR STATE EXAMS ALONE, IN A SMALL* room attached to the principal's office. I don't get to see the rest of the school or any of the kids.

I don't belong here anymore.

But I will come back this summer, along with Chad whether or not he wants me. We'll still be friends. I imagine his surprised look when I tell him we'll be in summer school together. Maybe even in the same classroom, once they discover I really know everything and can be his private tutor.

When the assistant principal instructs me, I open the first page of my test booklet. Algebra I.

#1: The equations $12x + 18y = 48$ and $18x + 18y = 63$ represent the money collected from the sale of cupcakes and doughnuts on two different days. If $x$ represents the cost of cupcakes, how much does each cupcake cost? (A) $1.00; (B) $1.50; (C) $2.00; (D) $2.50.

Easy. Cupcakes are $2.50. I darken the circle next to (A).

Every few times, I get one right. Missing every single question seems too deliberate.

I could have scored at least a 96 on the Algebra I exam. Instead, I'm getting a 45.

I work out every problem in my head so I know which circles are wrong and which are most likely to be because of a careless error. Where it says to show the work, I make the careless error. Like #1: Not reading the problem carefully enough. Or #3: Solving the equations in the wrong order.

About halfway through the test, I consider erasing all my wrong answers and putting the right ones in. It will be embarrassing to fail a test. I used to cry when I got below a 90. Ms. Latimer will say it's my fault for spending too much time making videos. She may change her mind and recommend me for the ED/LD class.

I know Dad will be angry with me. He's arranging to go on tour as an extra musician with a band after I leave, but now he'll have to stay home and work at Tech Town while I attend summer school. Too bad for him. He should have stood up for me and not let Mami take me away from my only friends.

Mami will be angry too, but it doesn't matter because she isn't coming home anyway. She's busy in Montreal with her new band and the famous singer. I don't think she misses me nearly as much as Mrs. Mac said she does. And now, Max—one of her normal children—is up there for the summer, playing keyboards with the band, while the other normal child, whose name I refuse to mention, has an internship in Boston.

I hand the assistant principal my answer sheet fifteen minutes early.

Next comes social studies.

#1: Farmers in the South who lived on land belonging to a large landowner, and who paid rent with part of their harvest rather than with money, were called (A) sodbusters; (B) migrants; (C) sharecroppers; (D) muckrakers.

Instead of (C), I fill in (A).

Unlike Algebra I, social studies has an essay portion. I'm supposed to interpret a cartoon about the Gilded Age and write a paragraph. I get the dates wrong and write about the Roaring Twenties.

I decide not to fail my science test. I'm already in summer school anyway for math and social studies. Science is my favorite subject. I could teach it, if Chad would only let me, and I can't see myself going over things I recite in my sleep.

I figure on a perfect 100 in science and 45 in Algebra I. I don't know about social studies because they could grade my essay easy. But I got wrong more than half the multiple choice and true-false questions.

Just before opening my English test, I think again about Dad and how he'll probably take away my computer forever. That would mean no classes with Mr. Internet. And no way to upload videos.

I can still meet Mr. Internet at the public library. *Hey, Dad, I'm going to the library to study. So I won't have to repeat eighth grade, you know.* Yes. That's what I'll tell him.

Since they don't let you make and upload YouTube videos at the library, I'll have to ask Antonio. As I guessed, he didn't mind when I told him that I lost my computer for not doing my homework. Veg offered to upload the videos to his computer and edit them for me, but his aren't getting as many hits as mine did. So I'm pretty sure Antonio will say yes to me coming over and using his computer.

I imagine myself with Antonio at his big, fancy house. Making sandwiches in the kitchen, everything shiny and clean, tile floors and granite countertops like in *Hogar*, the home-decorating magazine in Spanish Mami used to read. They keep sending it to us even though she's no longer here.

The assistant principal interrupts my thoughts. "Time's passing. You need to focus on the test."

I realize I've been staring at the clock. Twenty minutes have passed of my allotted hour. And, no, I can't hand in a blank page.

I start with the essays. This time, I answer the two questions, but I print so slowly and neatly that I have a work of art when the assistant principal calls time, but only a third of the little circles for the vocabulary and grammar parts filled in. At least when they read the essays, the people grading the test won't think I'm a complete idiot.

I smile and hand the assistant principal my answer sheets for the English exam. She wishes me a good summer.

I could write a book on how to fail the state exams on purpose.

# CHAPTER 22

**DAD HAS ARRANGED TO TAKE OFF WORK TO DRIVE ME TO** Montreal after my lessons with Ms. Latimer end. I wonder what he'll do when he finds out I can't go because I failed my exams and will have to attend summer school. I have ten days to wait before we find out my scores. Ms. Latimer has me do fun stuff like puzzles and board games. I stare at the unplugged computer and think about all the video footage in my camera that I need to edit and upload.

During the week Antonio tells me about a party he and his friends have organized at the BMX track on Saturday. He calls it the "end-of-school blowout" because he, Veg, and Brian are graduating high school the following Wednesday. He wants me to film everyone's stunts. I haven't been to a party since the disaster at Emily Stein's in fourth grade. But I expect to be grounded for a long time, and this might be one of my last chances to see all my friends.

The party starts at two on Saturday afternoon and is supposed to last all night. Dad's working until nine to make up for all the days he'll miss, so if I get home by then, I'm safe. I tell Chad to come over at one thirty so we can ride there together—me on Chad's bike, him on his BMX bike. I want to show up on a shiny, new bike, but mainly, I don't want to show up alone. I want all the people I don't know to see that I already have a friend.

Yet by two, there's no Chad. Not even his family's van in the driveway.

I'm *itching,* as Chad would say. Wasting time. Kids will be doing stunts and expecting me to film them. The thought of arriving alone makes my knees go shaky. I wipe my sweaty palms on my jeans and wheel Max's bike out of the lean-to. Before I can put on my backpack and helmet, I hear the van's peculiar cough.

*Yes!* I whisper to myself. I back the bike into the lean-to and run to my front porch to await Chad. Five minutes later, he rides up the street on his mountain bike, towing his BMX bike alongside him.

"Where were you?" I ask.

"McDonald's." He has a gauze bandage wrapped around his left forearm near his elbow, where he got a nasty turf burn bailing on a backflip yesterday. I check the saddlebags for two-liter bottles of churning chemicals. Empty. I stuff my rolled-up backpack with the camera, notebook, and pencil into a bag.

While stopped at a traffic light in downtown Willingham, Chad picks at the gauze. I tell him, "Veg wants to call your video 'Backflop.'"

"Not funny. I'm gonna do it perfect this time." Chad looks

away, toward the river. The light changes, and he takes off ahead of me, pedaling hard. I pump to catch up with him, hoping the effort will make my knees less shaky.

*Last-minute tutoring,* I think. *Maybe that will help.* "Hey, Chad. What am I supposed to do?" I shout.

He grunts and drops back behind me.

I slow to let him catch up and try again. "The party? What should I say?"

"Dunno. Be yourself."

*That's a lot of help.*

"Oh, yeah," he then says. "Make sure you get all my stunts."

When we get there, I check my watch. Three o'clock. We have nearly five hours until I have to go home. The area around the BMX track is already filled with kids wearing the red and black colors of College Park High School.

Veg trots toward us, waving both hands above his head.

"Yo, Raggy!" Veg calls out Chad's nickname—short for Raggedy Chad.

Antonio catches up to his friend. "If it isn't rogue266 and Gambit Double 360." He winks at me. I think he's figured out my obsession with the X-Men from my YouTube uploads even though I haven't actually told him. I smile back.

Veg lowers his voice and tells us, "Gotta show you the new ice chest we made."

Chad and I follow Veg and Antonio to a smaller clearing in the woods where some other high school kids stand in a circle, holding cans. They step aside to let us through. At our feet is a pit, three feet by three feet, lined with a shower curtain and filled with soda, beer, and ice.

"Cool!" Chad says.

"You dug that hole?" I ask. It makes me think of the holes I dug for Brandon's wrestlers, only a hundred times bigger.

"This morning. It's Mother Nature's ice chest." Antonio crouches down and grabs a can of soda. I do the same.

When Antonio isn't looking, Chad snatches a beer can from the hole, pops the top, and takes a long swallow. I gulp my soda. We're both sweaty from the ride and the almost-ninety-degree heat. And I'm not surprised to see Chad drinking. He's had beer with the other guys before, chugging his cans like someone who's been sneaking them from the refrigerator for years, which on one wobbly ride home he told me he did.

After Veg and some other kids scoop up cans, Antonio drags a sheet of plywood over the hole. Some of the kids drift away. Antonio and I walk through the woods in the opposite direction toward the creek. I smell pine sap mixed with perspiration. Mine. Antonio's. The buzz of many conversations fades the farther we get from the pit, replaced by the gurgle of water running past rocks.

I take the camera from the backpack to get some footage of the creek. I know I'll use it at some point. Running water always makes for cool images.

"Want me to interview you?" Antonio asks.

"Interview?"

He wriggles the camera out of my hand and points it at my face. "We're here with the world-famous videographer rogue266. Rogue, say hi to your fans."

"Hi, fans," I mumble, confused.

"A little more enthusiasm, okay?"

Louder, I repeat, "Hi, fans."

"Through image and music, you've captured the thrill of freestyle BMX and mountain biking. What's your secret?"

The words don't come. I shift from one foot to another. Gaze at the pine needles under my sneakers. *Keep the camera still? Never let the bike leave the frame? Zoom into his center the moment the rider takes to the air—and the moment he wipes out?*

"I . . . I can't," I say, looking away to the side.

"Sorry I put you on the spot." Antonio lowers the camera and hands it to me. After deleting his recording to avoid further embarrassment, I tuck it under my arm. "I guess great artists don't talk about their work," he says. "They just do it."

He's right. When I'm behind the camera, sitting in the grass overlooking the BMX track, I feel strong. Capable. Like I belong.

We return to the track. The sun is high, and shadows don't get in the way of my filming. The boys take turns doing their stunts while I record them. Even some girls ride the mounds. Chad gets a lot of attention for the perfect backflip that he practiced yesterday. *That trick is beast,* a couple of the other kids say. They all think he's really cool— or *beast,* which I guess means cool.

I write their names along with their stunts and a description of their bikes in my notebook. This way, I can match the riders with their videos. Some of the names I recognize from previous weeks, even though I don't recognize the faces.

Three hours later, the sun has dropped toward the horizon. I have to move around more for the best lighting to capture the expressions on the riders' faces and the details of their stunts. Fewer kids are riding because the glare messes with their moves, just as it washes out my picture if I aim the camera the wrong way.

Someone brings a stack of pizza boxes to the edge of the woods. Someone else refills the pit. Antonio brings me a slice of pepperoni on a paper plate.

"I'll take another soda," I tell him. People are eating now, not riding, and I have nothing else to do except stare at the empty track.

He comes back with a diet soda. I frown.

"You drink diet, don't you?" he asks.

"No. Not really."

"Sorry. I thought most girls—"

"It's okay," I interrupt. He ought to know by now I'm not like most girls. But I don't want to mess things up, so I pop the top instead.

With the first sip, I recoil at the fake sweetness. I force myself to drink more, then cover up the chemical aftertaste with a bite of pepperoni. Antonio sits on a patch of grass next to me. Suddenly, I feel dizzy. My mouth is dry. I take another swallow. I have to tell him about the test.

"Dad wants to send me to Montreal this summer," I begin.

"Max is there, right? It's cool you're staying with him."

*Cool? No, it's not cool.* "I flunked my state exams on purpose," I tell Antonio.

"No way," he says.

"So that I'll have to stay around and go to summer school. And I bet my dad'll ground me." Thinking about it makes my stomach do a backflip. A mouthful of soda sets it back where it belongs. "But you can come by and visit."

"Wow. Like a jail visit."

"Something like that."

Antonio leans in toward me. His breath is tangy. Sweet. "You're a big-time troublemaker. First getting kicked out of school, then getting your computer taken away for not doing your homework. Now this."

The lie about the homework, thrown back at me, makes me hesitate. *I have to keep track of the lies.* "Yeah, it was really weird. I used to never fail tests. Most of the time I got a hundred."

"So . . . *why?*" Antonio licks his lips. I wonder what it's like to kiss someone . . . on the lips? The backflips start up again.

*Under the influence of the Golgotha space creatures, Rogue and Wolverine kissed.*

Antonio stands up and moves to my other side. Does he know I wanted to kiss him? My gaze falls to his red muscle T-shirt, his bare arm, and the Livestrong tattoo.

"I wanted to stay with my friends," I say.

I touch Antonio's shoulder. His skin is hot. My arm stiffens, and a burning sensation spreads from my fingers all the way to my heart, as if instead of sucking out his emotions, he's sucking out mine. *He doesn't think what I did is cool. He thinks it's stupid and weird.* I let my hand drop into my lap. Heat flows out of my body. The swirling inside me stops.

Antonio taps my shoulder. "Did anyone ever tell you that you look like Anna Paquin?" he asks. When I look up, he brushes back the strands of hair that have come out of my ponytail.

"Really?" My voice comes out as a squeak. "You know she plays Rogue in the *X-Men* movie?" I twist around and notice the groups of kids walking toward us. "But I'm the real Rogue."

"Two-six-six." Antonio smiles at me—a big smile that I think means he cares about me.

I stand, brush the dirt from my jeans, and pick up my backpack. "Can we, like, walk somewhere?" I ask, not wanting the rest of the kids to hear about the X-Men and me.

"Sure."

When we get to the woods, I tell him about Rogue and Wolverine and Gambit, about needing to find my special power so I can make the world understand mutants and be nicer to us, and he listens to me. But I'm nowhere near finished when I hear a rustling.

I whirl around.

A husky-voiced "Boo!" makes me jump.

Chad steps out of the woods and stands in front of us, hands on his hips. He's not smiling.

# CHAPTER 23

ANTONIO DROPS HIS CAN. "WHAT THE . . . ?"

Soda spills out and soaks into the ground, leaving a puff of foam.

Chad lights into me. "You're supposed to be by the track, Kiara. Recording us."

"No one was riding. You were all eating." I glance at him, confused.

A muscular boy with short dark hair and a black College Park High School T-shirt jogs up to Chad and slaps his back. "Yeah, Raggy, what's with your girlfriend not recording you?"

Two boys and two girls join them. My watch tells me we only have forty minutes until I have to leave. The growing crowd and gloom of dusk tell me I may have lost my last chance to talk any more to Antonio.

"Know what you need, Little Man? Muscles like that dude. Then she'd want to take your picture." The kid with the black T-shirt pokes Chad in the chest. Chad only comes up to his shoulder, and he stumbles backward, arms flailing. The big kid laughs.

"Lay off him, Josh," a girl says. Her tight red T-shirt reads College Park Girls' Basketball. She musses Chad's hair.

"Check out those pencil arms," another boy says. He lifts Chad's unbandaged arm and squeezes his bicep.

Chad shakes loose from his group and stalks toward me. He spits to the side, inches from Antonio's feet.

"She's retarded, Wheezer. She lives for those stupid X-Men."

Antonio steps backward. "Chill, Raggy."

"Yeah, that's cold, calling her that," says the boy who squeezed Chad's arm. "No way to treat your girlfriend."

*Tell him, College Park kid. It's mean to call someone retarded.* I want to shout it myself, but I'm afraid of how my voice will sound. And if the others will call me Crybaby Kiara when they hear me.

"X-Men are sorta cool," someone says from the now-larger crowd.

"Not the way she's into them. And you . . ." Chad points a shaking finger at Antonio. "That's messed up, taking her away from what she's supposed to be doing to talk about comic books."

"Ooh, Little Man's the jealous type," another kid says.

"Gonna fight him for your girl?" The kid in the black T-shirt edges Chad forward, as if to get him to punch Antonio.

The others step back and form a semicircle around us.

They want a fight. Or maybe they want Antonio to teach Chad a lesson. Not to call me retarded or act like he's the boss of me. Antonio was my brother's friend and now my friend. I have a right to talk to him. And he acted like he wanted me to tell him about the X-Men.

Instead of going for Antonio, Chad pushes himself up into my face. I recoil from his sour beer breath. His face is flushed and glistening with sweat. "Chad, you're drunk. How much have you had already?"

He puffs out his chest. "Not as much as I'm gonna have."

The big kid in the black T-shirt, the one they call Josh, laughs. "This little guy can put it away. And still walk a straight line. Show her."

Chad turns from me and glares at Antonio, like he still wants to fight a kid six years older and nearly a foot taller. Another boy yells, "Yeah, show her, Raggy," and the other kids chant, "Raggy, Raggy, Raggy."

Chad whirls around and marches in a straight line, back to the pit. Antonio was right: I shouldn't have brought Chad to the trails in the first place.

Antonio grips my shoulder. "Take him home now. This isn't going to turn out well."

I frown at the thought of leaving Antonio. "Chad doesn't listen to me."

At the edge of the pit, Veg, Kevin, Brian, and some girls are passing around a thirty-two-ounce Gatorade bottle filled with a pink liquid. Chad slips into the group and snatches the Gatorade out of a girl's hand. He pinches his nose shut, tips his head back, and drains the bottle.

Then he shoves his way past the group and heads back to Antonio and me. "I hate you both!" he screams, and hurls the bottle straight at Antonio's head.

Antonio ducks, and the bottle flies over his head.

"Whoa," Veg says.

"How much was in the bottle?" Antonio asks.

"A quarter. Maybe a third." Veg shrugs. "Almost pure vodka."

"Someone should stick a finger down his throat. Before he croaks or something," Brian says.

But Chad is already running toward the bike track. All four of us take off after him. My pack with the camera thumps my shoulder blades. I don't know what Brian's talking about. Croaking. Like a frog.

Chad, now weaving and stumbling a bit, grabs the first bike. Not his beater but a shiny silver one. He climbs on, bounces on the seat, and pumps the pedals.

He has no helmet. He rides faster and faster around the perimeter of the pit. I stop at the grassy border, close enough to feel a musty breeze as he passes below and in front of me.

Behind me, someone says, "You have to get this one, Camera Girl. He's going to pull off the world's sickest stunt or die trying."

I drop my pack. None of the College Park kids called me retarded. They took my side. They want me to make their videos, and they want to be my friends.

Chad was supposed to be my tutor, but he acted mean and now he did something he shouldn't have done. If I tell him to stop riding—or at least to put on a helmet—he won't listen to me.

I scoop the camera out and set its aperture to its widest setting. Having filmed concerts, I get great images in dim light.

"Blaze of glory, you jerks," Chad yells. I train the camera on the circling bike. If I loop the footage, it'll make people as dizzy as Chad must be feeling right now. I smile at my brainstorm.

Going full speed, Chad zips up the mound closest to me and launches himself vertically into the air. The setting sun illuminates half his body, with the other half cast in darkness. *Hey, thanks for giving me the best shot,* I think. On his way up, he lets go of the bike. It sails forward. Chad keeps rising, spinning like a corkscrew—*light, dark, light, dark, light, dark.* His hair flies outward the way it flew when he spun with his feet on the ground in the park.

The bike crashes into the lip of the next mound and bounces into the pit between them. A boy curses behind me.

Chad levels out, arms and legs askew. As he dives, I zoom into the center of his body, focus on his T-shirt-covered belly full of vodka and beer, pizza and McDonald's. He flips and hits the top of the mound on his butt. He bounces a few feet into the air. Then he flops onto his stomach and rolls facedown, headfirst to the bottom of the mound. Dirt flies around him. He comes to a stop on his back, a quarter turn away from where the bike came to rest.

"What a wipeout!"

"Classic."

*At least ten thousand hits,* I think. The camera continues recording. Holding my hand steady, I walk slowly toward him.

For a long moment Chad doesn't move. Dirt sticks to his hair, mouth, and cheeks. One cheek is rubbed raw, specked with blood and dirt.

I feel the crowd gather behind me but keep my eye on the screen. Chad rocks back and forth, trying to get onto his side. After a few tries, he rolls onto his left side and touches his hand to his scuffed cheek.

Through the screen I see a thin line of liquid in the dirt next to his hip. The line becomes a river that puddles next to his thigh. The top part of his jeans is soaked.

"Peed his pants," someone says.

Chad lifts his head. His eyes are wide open and unfocused. He rolls onto his stomach and lifts himself onto his hands and knees. Pushing off from one knee, he struggles to his feet. He sways and staggers forward.

"Can't feel my legs," he says, the words running together.

"How was the ride?" I ask, camera still recording, setting sun to my side. I put on my interviewer tone, the way Antonio did when he tried to interview me.

Eyes shiny and rimmed with dirt, Chad thrusts his face toward the camera. "Haven't stopped."

He stumbles toward the fallen bike. I scoot in front of him, keeping the focus on his face but for a moment cutting to his wet and dirt-caked jeans. The image is too dark, but I can fix it later. "You wiped out. What was that like?"

"Din't . . . wipe . . . out." He hiccups. "In . . . air." He stretches out his arms. "Flying."

He hiccups again, licks his lips, and swallows. A groan rises from deep inside him, and he claps his hand to his mouth the moment before he crashes into the bike.

Pink liquid gushes from his mouth, followed by what looks like oatmeal and stinks like rotting garbage. I take a couple of steps back. Slime drips from the silver bike's frame and tires and pools underneath.

"That's my bro's bike you puked on!" The boy with the black T-shirt, Josh, sticks his palm in front of my camera. "I'm gonna kill that kid."

Chad straightens up. I hit the stop button.

"Kill me." He staggers toward Josh. "Don't . . . want . . . to . . . live." He drops onto his knees as if kneeling to pray.

# CHAPTER 24

JOSH WAVES HIS HAND IN FRONT OF HIS FACE. "MAN, YOU stink," he says.

"Hey, Camera Girl," someone else calls out. "Why'd you turn it off?"

"Don't you know people like watching stupid drunks?"

"Extra points if you catch 'em puking."

I do what they ask even though I already have the extra points—raise the camera and get Chad and Josh on my screen. I hit the record button right before Josh puts his hand on Chad's shoulder and pushes him hard into the ground. Chad cries out. I can't make out his words because of all the talking behind me.

My hand trembles. I fight to hold the camera steady. Chad sprawls on his side. Josh steps up to him. "Raggy, you are *banned* from here."

Then he steps forward, pivots, and kicks Chad in the stomach. The thud of impact mixes with the gasps of kids behind me. My own gasps. Chad's breath rushes out in a strangled moan. He curls up in a tight ball. Josh circles him like he's about to kick him again.

*Josh . . . no!* I want to scream, but I can't. Josh is big and Chad is small. Josh has friends, and Chad has none. Just a bunch of people watching him do stupid things.

Like me.

Until now, I was glad the kids were picking on someone else and not me. And Chad deserved it for what he called me. *But I can be next.* I don't belong here either. I don't live in College Park or go to the high school. I do stupid things all the time.

My ears fill with the noise of a dozen conversations, Chad whimpering, Josh yelling at Chad. Then Veg and Antonio break through the crowd. They rush at Josh and pull him away, each holding an arm. Josh breaks free from Veg's grip and takes a swing at him.

Antonio . . . saving Chad from getting picked on?

"Fight!"

The heat of the big kids and their odors of cologne and sweat and beer press in on me.

My face burns. My eyes blur. Antonio's Livestrong tattoo appears sharp in my mind. He and Veg are doing what I should have done. "Stop it! All of you!" I yell.

I spin around. Orange light flashes in my screen. I do a reverse quarter turn and record them—all the people who've stood watching.

Except for me.

I'm the invisible one.

Rogue would have thrown fireballs to save Gambit. Didn't matter that they'd just argued with each other because they argued all the time. They came from the same place and were best friends.

*How many times did Gambit say he hated Rogue?*

*How many times did she rescue him anyway?*

In the face of my camera, the kids scatter. Brian and Kevin pin Josh's arms behind him and drag him away. He kicks out at them.

But it's too late. Chad's whimpers turn to gurgles and gasps. Then silence.

I stand frozen, my back to Chad, staring into the woods. The low sun has turned the tree trunks golden against a mosaic of greens. I slip the camera's shoulder strap over my head and punch the stop button.

I'm not Rogue. I can't save Chad like she saved Gambit.

"Oof!"

I twist around. Antonio holds Chad upright, one fist atop the other against the smaller boy's stomach. Like he's doing the Heimlich maneuver.

Like he's Wolverine bolting to the rescue.

Color rushes to Chad's ashen face. Chunks of pizza and more liquid pour from his mouth onto his T-shirt and Antonio's bare arms. Onto his own limp arms, soaking the bandage. When he stops, his head droops and his tongue hangs from his mouth. He grabs for his stomach.

"Get his feet," Antonio says. "We have to take him home."

Holding my breath, I slide my hands under the rolled-up cuffs of Chad's jeans and grab his bare ankles. Sticky, still-warm puke covers his sneakers and the bottoms of his jeans. His head flops backward over Antonio's tattoo.

"We can't. Not with his parents cooking there," I say. We start walking, away from the other kids and toward the part of the woods where I left Chad's mountain bike.

"Right." Antonio shifts the deadweight in his arms. "I can't carry him much farther. We'll have to get the guys to help once Josh calms down. And find a ride because I came on my bike."

It's getting dark fast. I don't want to stay in the woods any longer with all the wild animals and the party still going on. In the distance, even more kids are arriving, flashlights in hand. We're the only ones leaving.

"Can we take him to your place?" I ask Antonio—even though Chad would mess up the huge, spotless house that I've imagined.

Antonio shakes his head. "No way. My mom's boyfriend is there. And he's . . ."

"He's what?" I'd never imagined anyone else living in Antonio's house. He never talked about his mother.

Antonio lowers his voice. "The dean of the university." He hitches Chad's shoulders toward him. Chad groans. "Scandal City if we turn up there."

I have to do something. To keep Antonio from a scandal. To find a place where we can take care of Chad until he sobers up, because Antonio already saved him from choking, and even if Chad acted like a jerk, I don't want him to die. But if I do my part, I'll get into even more trouble than I'm going to get into when Dad finds out I failed my exams on purpose. "I can call Dad at work. But I don't have a phone."

Antonio sets Chad down next to the bike, wipes his hands on the seat of his cargo pants, and digs his cell phone from the side pocket. It's a much more expensive model than Dad's and it takes me a few seconds to figure it out.

"Hello."

I take a deep breath. "Dad. It's me. We need your help. We're in College Park. In the woods behind the sledding hill, and Chad . . . he's"—I look down at the grimy, smelly hunched-over boy I thought of as Gambit—"he's hurt bad."

## CHAPTER 25

VEG HELPS US CARRY CHAD TO WHERE THE TRAIL MEETS THE
road, and Brian follows us with Chad's two bikes, a few
bottles of water, and a handful of paper napkins. After they
leave, Chad crawls into the woods to throw up. Antonio
goes with him to make sure he doesn't choke again. I hold
the phone in case Dad gets lost. Text messages scroll past:
*u coming back?* from Brian G, *howz raggy?* from Veg, *im
gonna get u loser* from J Laiken.

Veg is worried about Chad. Someone's mad at Antonio.
Could J Laiken be Josh?

All the effort seems to wake Chad up and makes him
fidgety too. He picks at his stained bandage, then unrolls
it. Underneath the inflamed skin oozes.

"Does it hurt?" I ask him.

"My stomach hurts." He sniffs. "Why did he kick me?"
His words are so slurred I can barely make them out.

Antonio answers, "'Cause you barfed on his brother's
bike."

I glance quickly at Antonio, his face now dark in the twilight. I may be slow to understand things, but that's still a rotten excuse to kick a smaller kid.

Antonio's phone plays a rap song. He punches a button and lifts it to his ear. "Hello . . . Mr. Thornton? . . . This is Antonio Baran. Max's friend. Kiara and Chad are with me. . . . Are you on State Route Twelve? . . . It's one mile past the Highway Six overpass. Beresford Road entrance to Beresford Estates . . . No, you've gone too far. Turn around."

Chad moans. I shush him, I want to hear everything, but only Antonio's side comes through.

"Kiara's fine. Chad had a fight, though. It wasn't his fault. Some kid went off on him."

Antonio faces the street, where lines of cars are parked on both sides, as far as I can see. A couple walks toward us, arm in arm.

"Yes, there was drinking. Not Kiara, though," Antonio says. The couple passes us without a word of greeting. "Are you at Beresford Road now? . . . Go all the way to the end of the road. You can't miss the cars."

Two minutes later, the lights of Dad's truck blind me. He and Antonio load the bikes in first and tie them down. No one talks, but Chad mumbles softly. We lift him to the back of the truck and pull him across the bed.

Antonio and I crouch low and hang on to the bikes in silence while Dad drives. We couldn't have heard each other anyway, with the wind and road noise.

"I'm surprised your dad didn't bite my head off," Antonio says at a traffic light.

"He doesn't bite," I say. "He's way too old."

"I don't mean that." Antonio smiles for a second. "He's taking it a lot more calmly than my mom would."

"Or mine. But Dad isn't the flipping-out type." More like the do-nothing type, according to Mami. But right now, I'm grateful that my dad is so mellow.

When we get home, Dad tells us to bring Chad upstairs to the bathroom, then goes inside to make coffee. Antonio tries to carry Chad through the back door, but he stretches out his arms and kicks at Antonio while shouting, "Leave me outside!"

"Fine with me," Antonio says as he sets Chad on the back step. It's fine with me too. I don't want to bring Chad in smelling like he does. While Antonio stays with him, I dig out some of the clothes my brothers left behind— boxer shorts, sweatpants, a science fair T-shirt, and a T-shirt from the Willingham High School marching band. Two sets—for Antonio as well as for Chad. I take soap, shampoo, hydrogen peroxide, and gauze from the bathroom and go downstairs.

Outside, under the porch light, Antonio holds Chad's head up while Dad tips the coffee mug to his mouth. "Why don't you let him sleep?" I ask. "Now he's going to be hyper all night."

"I'd like him to sober up a bit first."

"I'm sorry we made you leave work early," I mumble. "Maybe you can make it up . . ." I stop myself before saying *next week*.

Dad grunts. "We'll talk about it tomorrow."

"I'm not in trouble, am I?" I realize I sound like a little kid—in front of Antonio. Hot blood rushes to my face.

"I don't know what to think," Dad snaps. Of course I didn't tell him I was going to a party, and he certainly wouldn't have suspected it. Why would he? I haven't been invited to a party in years.

After Chad finishes the coffee, I turn on the hose and spray him. Even though it's a warm evening and he's full of hot coffee, he shivers. His dark lips stand out on his face. Dad goes inside for a blanket.

"I'm going to set things straight with your father." Antonio folds his arms across his chest and lets his breath out slowly. "He was right, what he said on the phone. You two had no business at a high school party in another town."

Still, I don't want to think of my first party in four years as a giant mistake like the other one. "You had fun riding, didn't you, Chad?"

He nods weakly.

"And I'm going to make some great videos. Right?" But when I look at them, I'm the only one smiling.

Antonio takes a set of dry clothes and pushes them toward Chad. "Can you get dressed by yourself?" he asks.

Chad fumbles with a wet T-shirt that sticks to his body.

"Okay, raise your arms, little buddy," Antonio says.

Chad holds both arms straight up. I step to his other side and into the foul musk that still clings to him despite my efforts with the hose. When we pull the T-shirt inside out over Chad's head, I gasp. Across his pale back are crisscrossed scars and welts.

Chad must have heard me. "Wha?" he asks.

"What happened to your back?"

"I fell."

I turn away while Antonio helps him into Max's sweatpants.

*He didn't fall. Scrapes from wipeouts don't look like that.*

Chad sags against Antonio, who helps him to sit down again and then sits next to him. I sit on Chad's other side.

I imagine us as Rogue, Gambit, and Wolverine, seated side by side in the X-Mansion after Rogue and Wolverine rescued the injured Gambit. They made sure he stayed with the X-Men and didn't return to his family of thieves.

Antonio leans forward, his head in his hands. My Wolverine doesn't know what to do. But I think he was wrong about Chad being trouble. Chad's family forced him to do what he did and beat him if he didn't.

"Do they hit Brandon too?" I ask.

"No." Chad's voice weakens. "I make sure of that."

"You protect him?"

Chad nods. "I'm ruined. But he should have a good life."

"You're not ruined."

"Yeah, I am. Look at me. I'm gonna run away with Brandon 'fore they do it to him."

I blink. How can Chad be ruined when he cares so much for his brother?

Chad burps, then mumbles, "I don't feel so good."

I hear and feel footsteps behind me. Dad pokes Antonio with a plastic bucket. Antonio jerks upright, grabs it, and holds it in front of Chad in time to catch a rush of sour coffee.

Dad crouches behind Chad and rubs his back. Chad flinches and moans.

"Careful, Dad. His back is all beat up."

My father rests a hand on Chad's bony shoulder, holding him steady. "I heard you talk about it."

Which means he heard how Chad took the blows for Brandon. "So what can we do to help them?" I ask.

If my father were Professor X, he would do something. But I'd never thought of Dad as a superhero. So when he says, "I'm going to have to speak to some people. This can't go on," I don't know if I believe him.

What Dad can do: Clean and rebandage Chad's arm. Put him to bed in Max's bottom bunk. That's it. Half an hour later, someone picks Antonio up. He won't tell me who. I go upstairs to my room.

The next morning, when I peek into my brothers' room to check on him, Chad is snoring. Back in my room on the opposite side of the house, I glance out the window, half-expecting Dad and Mr. Elliott to jam in the park with their guitar and banjo even though it's only seven thirty, still too early for them to get together. I wonder what Dad will say to Mr. Elliott about last night.

Around nine, Brandon comes outside. Is he waiting for Chad to come home? Should I go to the park and tell him what happened and that his brother's all right?

While I'm changing from my pajamas into a shirt and jeans, a police car with two officers inside drives down Washington Avenue. The car stops across from the park and idles for a couple of minutes. Squinting, I see one cop hold up what looks like a clipboard. Brandon runs inside his house. But instead of getting out of their car, the cops pull back into traffic and out of my view.

*Brandon didn't need to run inside. They weren't looking for the Elliotts. They're just passing through.*

Someone knocks hard on our front door. *The cops? Looking for us?* Legs trembling, I run downstairs right behind Dad, who is already dressed. "That was fast," he mumbles.

"What's so fast?" I ask him, but get no answer.

Dad opens the door. Two police officers stand on the other side. They show their badges. One says, "We're looking for Jeremy Thornton. He reported a case of child abuse."

My chest tightens. I can't breathe. *Dad called the cops?*

A brief flash of light comes from behind me, from the park, and an explosion shatters the air. The entire house rocks. My hands fly to the top of my head. The two cops take off running.

# CHAPTER 26

**TWO MORE EXPLOSIONS RATTLE THE HOUSE. DUST FILLS THE** room. My eyes sting. Along with the dust are the odors— the intense onion smell from the Elliotts' entryway, the rotting-egg smell of their backyard, the fertilizer smell of Brandon's hair.

I try to clear my lungs. Dad is coughing too. "Let's go! Now!" he gasps. His hand squeezes my wrist.

My feet stay frozen in place. "What about Chad!" I choke out as Dad pulls me through the front door.

"He's safe upstairs."

Outside, sirens close in on us from all directions. Our house stands intact, but beyond the oak and pine trees, black smoke billows, and flames shoot high into the air above Mrs. Mac's house. Fire trucks pull up to the house, sirens screaming. Then police cars and ambulances arrive, red and blue lights flashing.

Hoses crisscross both Washington Avenue and Cherry Street. I cover my nose and mouth with the rolled-up sleeve of my shirt to filter the chemical stench. Dad approaches a policeman who's herding neighbors to the park.

"Did they get out?" Dad yells above the din.

"Stand back, sir."

"A little boy lives here. Did you find him?"

"Stand back, sir."

I gaze at the second floor engulfed in fire and smoke. A hose shoots water through the window above the side door, where the Mackenzies' dining room used to be.

Where is Brandon? I saw him run into the house, just before the police officers knocked on our door.

"Did you see the little boy who lives downstairs?" I ask two cops on the sidewalk. "He was my friend."

The officers' walkie-talkies drown me out. Someone calls, "Person down, behind the garage," and one of the cops dashes across the street.

"Going to get someone now," the other cop says. He holds his arm out, keeping me away.

An orange-and-white ambulance backs up. Emergency workers surround a stretcher. Two wheel it into the street and a third holds a bag with a tube at the bottom. Before they roll the stretcher into the ambulance, I get a glimpse of who's propped upright on it.

It's a man. Mr. Elliott?

The flames have singed his long hair almost to the scalp. A mask covers his nose and mouth. He holds up one arm, and it looks like all four of his fingers have melted away, leaving only a black-tipped thumb.

The siren screeches as the ambulance drives off.

Then another ambulance rolls into its place. Its crew pours out, carrying a freshly made-up stretcher-bed. Its sheets are clean, white. Within minutes, a stretcher with Mrs. Elliott is wheeled toward the ambulance. Her hair is burned too, and there's only black nothingness where her ear should be.

Dad lays his arm across my shoulders. I stiffen. I'm afraid to ask him about Brandon. His parents have been horribly burned. I imagine him burned too. But maybe . . . he escaped. He's a little kid. He can crawl through small spaces. And his bedroom's on the other side of the house. Maybe that side didn't burn as badly.

Dad shakes his head slowly. "I can't get any information about Brandon."

My teeth chatter despite the heat. "I saw him run inside. Right before the cops knocked on our door."

"They still think Chad's inside too. Even though I tried to tell them . . ."

Little by little, the water from the hoses knocks down the fire. The smoke turns gray, but the chemical smell hangs in the air, and the empty feeling stays inside me. Another ambulance pulls up, but its lights and sirens are turned off. It waits, engine idling, back doors open.

My father jogs up to the EMTs. Cops fan out in the brush behind the Mackenzies' yard and on the far side of the house. I listen to the crackle of emergency radios. Dad returns, shaking his head. "Brandon's still missing. But at least they know Chad's accounted for." He rubs my back. I shudder.

"I'm not leaving till they find Brandon." I *have* to play wrestlers with him again. Even if all his wrestlers got burned up, I'll come up with the money to buy him new ones.

"I agree. Chad will want to know." Dad pauses. "*I* want to know."

A few neighbors drift away after one of the cops calls us "a bunch of looky-loos," but then more come. The twins, Eddie and Mike Perez, arrive with their parents, who talk to one of the cops and then hustle the boys away. Channel 8 News shows up in a van with a satellite dish on top. Reporters jump out to interview people. I can hardly hear above the noise, the radios, the conversations, the vehicles, the sirens. An ambulance roars by on the avenue. A helicopter hovers.

*Police say . . . a meth lab . . . Did you suspect something?*

*We had no idea.*

*They just moved in.*

*They kept to themselves.*

*Two young boys . . . little one's a cutie.*

*The kids played in the park . . . there was music . . . in the park.*

I turn away from the cameras, because I don't want them to film me crying. I don't need the entire state calling me Crybaby Kiara even though this time I have a good reason to cry.

My father pushes his way through the crowd. He dodges a reporter holding out a microphone. "Kiara! Kiara!" he calls.

I wave. I can't tell from his face whether he has bad news or good news. Or any news at all. But someone told the reporter, *Little one's a cutie.* Like he still *is.*

When he gets to me, Dad's lips turn up at the ends. A smile. The skin around his eyes crinkles.

"Brandon?" I ask.

"They found him in the brush behind the house!"

"He's okay?"

"Not okay. But he's alive," Dad tells me. "The police officer told me Brandon has serious burns, but they aren't life-threatening."

*Burned like his parents?* I shiver, thinking how awful they looked.

"But he *will* get better, Kiara."

"You're sure?"

"He's on his way to the hospital now." Dad nudges me toward home. "He's in good hands."

I breathe out. It feels like the first breath I've taken since the explosion.

"We need to tell Chad. He'll be happy to hear his brother made it out," I say.

We come home to a silent house. Dad calls for Chad.

No answer.

Dad runs up the stairs, two at a time. By the time I get to the top, Dad's already in my brothers' room. The door is wide open and I hear Chad's voice, weak and groggy. "What's going on? And where am I?"

I stand in the open doorway. Huddled on the bottom bunk, Chad faces me. His skin is greenish-gray.

Dad sits next to him, hunched over to avoid hitting his head on the top bunk. "You're at Kiara's house. You had too much to drink last night. We brought you here where you'd be safe." Dad helps Chad to a sitting position, then reaches forward and drags a wastebasket toward the bed. "But there was an accident at your house this morning."

"What kind of accident?"

"A fire."

Chad pulls his legs up to his chest. His lips are cracked and crusted white. His eyes stare blankly into space. It occurs to me that his eyes are sky blue. Like an empty sky.

"Brandon?" he whispers. "Was he burned?"

"Yes, but he got out of the house before getting hurt too badly. The police found him in the brush behind your yard," my father says.

"He *will* get better," I add, repeating Dad's words to me.

I expect Chad to smile like Dad did when he found out the news that Brandon made it out alive. But Chad doesn't smile. Instead he says, "But he's *burned*."

My father pats Chad's back gently. "Yes. They took him to the hospital. Your parents too."

Chad squeezes his head between his knees. "I should have been the one that got burned." His voice breaks.

"You should be happy," I say, stepping into the room. "Brandon's going to be okay. And you're free from your evil parents." They'll never be able to snatch Chad back the way Gambit's parents snatched him back.

I don't know why both my father and Chad are staring at me, their mouths wide open.

In the silence, I continue. "But it's true!"

Dad leans forward. "That's enough, Kiara."

I stomp my foot and give Dad the open-mouthed stare.

Chad buries his fingers in his hair, like he's going to yank his hair out. "Why Brandon? He didn't do nothing to no one." Chad's voice is tiny and hoarse. Suddenly, he slams both his fists against his head, over and over. And then he howls.

# CHAPTER 27

*IN THE AFTERNOON, A WOMAN PULLS UP IN A COUNTY CAR TO* talk to Dad. Dad calls Chad downstairs but tells me I can't listen. I fold my arms across my chest and blow my breath out. I want to know if Brandon will be all right and where Chad is going now that he has no home and no family, and all his clothes and everything else have burned.

"Control yourself, Kiara," Dad whispers. "This is no time for a tantrum."

I glance at Chad. His head hangs, but I see the tears slick on his face. I escape through the backyard and the fence to watch the firemen spray water on piles of smoldering embers. The reporters and cops have left, except for one car with swirling lights blocking the entrance to Cherry Street. Orange cones and yellow biohazard tape surround the house and the sidewalk. The firemen stand outside the tape.

I walk behind the firemen, past their truck along the curb of Washington Avenue. The Ned Lamont sign lies flat on the ground, stomped and soggy. All that's left of the house is the first-floor extension, where the entrance to the record store used to be. Where the upstairs bedroom was, where Mr. Mac had his heart attack . . . nothing.

One of the firemen turns to me. "Hey, kid, you don't want to be out here. This smoke is toxic."

I'm immune. Contaminated by toxic chemicals before I was born. I keep walking up Washington Avenue.

I wipe my stinging eyes on my shirttail. As I gaze into the stand of trees and brush at the far side of the house, I imagine Brandon running there after the explosion, the back of his T-shirt aflame. That's what Dad told me—his shirt had melted into his back. It must have really hurt, even though Mr. Internet once told me the worst burns don't hurt because even the nerves are dead.

The biohazard tape keeps me from going into the brush, as if I could find my answers if I walked the path along which Brandon fled. I double back toward the park. Lying in the grass next to the burned house are bits and pieces of a family's life. A pot with a melted handle. A pair of metal scissors. What look like tuna fish cans, but blackened and without labels. And next to the curb, a half-dozen scattered wrestlers.

Brandon's wrestlers. "Brandon's hurt," I whisper to them, pushing the words past the clog in my throat. "Maybe you can help him feel better."

I collect the wrestlers, one by one, and cross the street. When I find out which hospital Brandon is in, I can bring them to him. And the new ones I buy for him too.

Then I see it, lying across two branches of the large oak

tree, right above the top of the fence. Mr. Elliott's banjo. It must have gotten blown out of the house in the explosion and landed in the tree branches above my backyard. A sign like Brandon's wrestlers? But only if the banjo isn't ruined.

I dash inside for the video camera. No one's in the kitchen. I hear voices, Dad's and the woman's, in the living room. The word *relatives* comes through, and then Dad.

"Chad Senior said they came from Iowa. He didn't say where. It's a big state."

Chad will go away too. I am sure about that. They'll send my Gambit to Iowa. Not New Orleans with the bayous and cypress trees, but a flat, dry place of cornfields and tornadoes.

I shut the back door quietly so they won't notice me. I locate the banjo in the camera screen and zoom in. The long neck is dull gray under the overcast sky. No dents or dings in it or the wooden resonator, and no cracks in the frosted white head. I take a few shots from different angles. Then I drag a ladder from the lean-to, prop it against the fence, and climb up. I sit atop the fence with my heels on the horizontal rail. Pulling the banjo out of the tree is like lifting a baby from a grown-up's arms. I hold it like a guitar and strum it a few times, but I can't play anything because my right hand and left hand don't work together. It's one of the ways I'm a mutant in a family of musicians.

I hide the banjo behind a pair of speakers and a microphone stand in the pantry. Dad will think the skinny neck is just another mike stand.

I will give Chad the banjo before he leaves so he'll remember me. He's the New Kid who stayed my friend the longest.

Chad refuses to eat dinner that night. He says his head and stomach hurt. Dad gives him some Tylenol and tells him to sip from the glass of water so pills and water stay down. And Chad will sleep instead of crying all night or whatever a kid does when his whole family gets blown up while he's passed out drunk at someone else's house.

Chad's asleep in Max's bottom bunk when Mami calls. Dad sends me to my room so he can talk to her downstairs.

"No!" I stomp my foot. "I want to hear what you say about me."

"Kiara, you're making things worse for yourself."

I fold my arms across my chest. "Then give me my cord back so I can use the computer."

Dad gives in. He retrieves the cord from his bedroom and hands it to me. But the computer's still downstairs where he won't let me go. *Stupid me,* I think as I bang my head softly on the wall next to my bed.

After giving myself a headache, I try to listen. A few words floating up from time to time tell me that they will send Chad to Iowa or to some place called a foster home, and I'll never see him again.

Finally, Dad hands me the phone. It's been nearly an hour and his battery is in the red.

"I'm sorry about the little boy that you babysat," Mami says. "I hope he gets better soon."

*I didn't babysit him. He was my friend.* I don't correct

her because she'll think it's weird that I play with little kids. She already thinks it's weird that I play with toys.

"And I hope they find a good home for him and your friend. So they can stay together."

I think of the unfamiliar words I heard. "*¿Qué es un* foster home?"

"Your father said they're looking for the boys' family first."

"They're in Iowa."

Mami sighs. "I'm praying for them. That someone can find the relatives. Their people must be worried about them."

The battery beeps, and I forget what I wanted to say.

"I've missed you so much, Kiara," Mami says.

"I . . . miss you too, Mami." Now I remember. She didn't answer my question about the foster home.

"I know you'll love Montreal. Now that you're older, there's so much we can do together."

"Mami, how do you say 'foster home' in Spanish?"

"*Casa de acogida.*" She pauses. "We can work on your Spanish too. And your French. You're lucky to be so talented with languages."

I smile. She wants me. She thinks I have a special talent, which is almost as good as a special power. At least it's a way I can make her proud of me.

But then my smile fades because of the state exams that I failed on purpose. When she finds out, she'll remember I'm the mutant she shouldn't have had.

# CHAPTER 28

*VIDEO OF THE BURNING HOUSE LEADS CHANNEL 8'S ELEVEN* o'clock news.

I try to tune out the pleasant voice of the anchorwoman, telling me once again what I saw with my own eyes—that Mr. and Mrs. Elliott got third-degree burns on their heads and arms. And what I didn't see—that Brandon got third-degree burns on his back and broke his arm while trying to escape. Dad never lets me stay up for the late news, but tonight he didn't make an attempt to send me to bed.

Right away I learned that Brandon had recently turned six—which means somewhere in the ruins is the Steel Cage Ring that Chad bought him for his birthday.

The TV cuts to a school picture. Brandon has a huge smile that shows his missing baby teeth. I don't have to touch the photo with skin and eyes and hair to feel as empty as Ms. Marvel did after Rogue touched her and stole her emotions.

The picture fades, replaced by the anchorwoman.

*Brandon was transferred by helicopter to a pediatric burn unit out of state where he is expected to recover. His parents, Chad and Melissa Elliott, are listed in critical condition at University Medical Center. Police believe that they were operating a meth lab out of their rental house, and when officers arrived at the neighborhood to investigate a child abuse report, the Elliotts disposed of the chemicals by pouring them down a drain. Police expect to charge both tomorrow on a variety of felony counts.*

A mug shot of Mr. Elliott flashes on screen. His hair is a lot darker than I remember.

Wait . . .

How could the police have taken this mug shot for his court case tomorrow if he's burned up in the hospital? I shudder at the image of his melted fingers.

*According to police, Chad Elliott previously served three years, from 1996 to 1999, in the Iowa state penitentiary for the manufacture and distribution of methamphetamine . . .*

That makes it a really old mug shot. I scoot closer to see what else might be different about Mr. Elliott. Not much. The same hollow cheeks. He had a sore on his lower lip then that wasn't there when he played music with Dad.

*Police originally believed the Elliotts' older son, twelve-year-old Chad Junior, was also in the house, but he was later found safe at a neighbor's house. He remains there, awaiting further arrangements.*

The TV cuts back to the fire and rescue workers running around.

*The explosion rocked the quiet neighborhood around*

*nine this morning. Neighbors say the owner of the house, Diane Mackenzie, recently relocated to Philadelphia . . .*

I glance up at the ceiling. Had Chad been there and not here . . . had Mrs. Mac not moved because she saw her husband's ghost . . . had Dad not called the police . . .

I wonder if Dad's thinking the same thing because he stares down at his hands and his carefully clipped guitar player's fingernails. I push one of Brandon's wrestlers back and forth across the wooden floor.

Old Mr. Toomey, who lives two houses up Cherry Street, is now talking into the Channel 8 microphone.

*"No, the wife and I, we had no idea what was going on. We often saw the boys playing in the park . . ."*

"No, they didn't play in the park," I shout at the TV, my voice breaking. "Their parents made them stand lookout there."

Dad makes a shushing sound and glances up at me. "I want to hear this, Kiara."

Mrs. Alvarado, the neighbor on the other side of Mr. Toomey, now appears on the screen.

*"They kept to themselves . . . No, there wasn't a lot of noise, and not a lot of people coming or going either. That's why we never suspected anything."*

And Mr. Toomey.

*"They just moved in. I don't think anyone really got to know them."*

The two anchors appear again. *Tomorrow on Live at Five: Experts discuss how to spot a meth lab in your neighborhood—and what to do about it.*

Dad has turned away from me. While the anchorman reads the national news, I spread what's left of Brandon's wrestlers on the floor and sort them into the good guys and the bad guys.

A Tech Town commercial comes on. I glance at the table in the corner of the living room, where my computer used to be. After I hung up with Mami, Dad carried all its pieces one by one to my bedroom. The first thing I asked Mr. Internet as soon as I plugged in the power cord was "what happens to kids who don't have a home?" because I wanted to find out where Chad would go after I left—and Brandon as soon as he got out of the hospital.

They would first look for a relative to take him in. If they couldn't find one, there are foster homes with loving parents who know how to help a kid who's had a terrible life.

Mami may not know, but Mr. Internet knows what foster homes are. *Loving parents who know how to help a kid . . .* That means Chad and Brandon would get to live in a better place. But they might end up somewhere far away—and no longer my friends.

After a mattress commercial, the anchors reappear on the screen.

*In other police news, more than a dozen teenagers have been arrested following an underage drinking party in College Park last night. Two students from the high school were treated at area hospitals for alcohol poisoning . . .*

I let the wrestler slip from my hand.

Alcohol poisoning? Is that what happened to Chad? And should he have gone to the hospital?

Then the police would have met Dad there. They wouldn't have come to our neighborhood, and Brandon wouldn't have run inside.

*Nineteen-year-old Stephen Nickolaus . . .*

Veg. My gut twists.

*. . . and eighteen-year-olds Brian Gerardi and Joshua Laiken were among those arrested and charged with trespassing, aggravated alcohol possession, and unlawful dealing with minors.*

I cover my face, but I can't block out Veg and Brian and Josh standing next to the height chart, all of them over the six-foot mark.

*The other suspects, all under eighteen years of age, have been released to their parents and their cases remanded to juvenile court. More arrests are expected as the investigation continues.*

I grip one of the wrestlers to steady my hand, but it still shakes. *The investigation continues* . . . Does that mean they arrested Antonio? I don't know who picked him up from my house, or if he returned to the party, or if evil Josh ratted him out.

Does that mean I'm next? I shot a video of Chad drunk.

I think about my phone call with Mami. She sounded excited to see me.

If I go to Montreal, I won't have to worry about the police coming after me for being at the party and making videos. I won't have to look at the burned-out house on the other side of the park where Mr. and Mrs. Mac and Chad and Brandon used to live.

My hand steadies. I scoop up the remaining wrestlers. Chad wanted to run away with Brandon. Now is my chance to run away, too. To start over somewhere else.

I smile at the thought. I won't be Crybaby Kiara or Crazy Kiara in Montreal, and Mami can tell me how to act so I make new friends. Because for the first time in my life, I'll be the New Kid.

Dad hits the remote control, and the TV goes black. "I think we've seen enough trouble," he says. When I don't answer, he adds, "Let's go to bed. Tomorrow is another day."

Tomorrow is another day. The day Ms. Latimer arrives with my test scores.

# CHAPTER 29

THE FIRST WORD MS. LATIMER SAYS TO ME WHEN SHE arrives is "why?" She tells Dad and me that I failed every one of the state exams except science. On that one, I received a perfect score.

"I like science," I answer.

"Don't. Smartmouth. Me," she says.

"Kiara . . ." Dad's voice is like a rumbling echo.

But I didn't smartmouth her. She asked me why I scored so well on the science test when I did so badly on the others.

Dad examines the piece of paper with my results. "There must be a mistake. She's never failed anything."

But there isn't a mistake. I made sure of that. And now I have to take it back.

"I'm as surprised as you are," Ms. Latimer tells my father. "We ran the multiple-choice answer sheets through the Scantron twice. But she didn't answer entire sections, and her essays had errors as well." She casts a glance in my direction. I look away. "It seems as if she was trying to fail."

Dad steps toward me. "Kiara, did you *want* to fail those exams?"

Eyes fixed on my shoelaces, I answer, "Yes." And then I think of the party and my videos, and the words pour out. "It wasn't because of you, Ms. Latimer. You were a good teacher. Dad was going to send me away for the summer, but I didn't want to go because I didn't want to leave my friends." I take a breath and rush to speak before Dad or Ms. Latimer stops me. "But now my friends are going away and the police are coming for me because of the party, so please let me retake the test. Please. I promise I won't flunk it this time."

"The police?" Ms. Latimer and Dad say at the same time. Jinx.

"Yeah, uh . . ." My hands shake. How do I explain that I shot a video of a lot of underage drinking?

Dad covers his face with his hands and then runs his fingers through his hair. "Ms. Latimer and I need to discuss this. Without you. Please take those bags up to Chad and wait in your room until we're done." He waves his hand toward a half-dozen bags of clothes and toys for Chad that the neighbors brought over this morning.

"Why can't I listen if it's about me?"

Dad's voice is hard. Mean. "Because it's not your decision. You've made a lot of decisions recently, and they haven't been good ones. Your teacher and I are going to decide what we think will be the best for you."

"Don't send me to juvie. They'll stick a knife in me."

"Calm down, Kiara. No one said you're going to juvie," Ms. Latimer says.

"I was at that party. In College Park. Dad had to pick me up from there."

"I doubt they're looking for you. They're probably looking for the kids who brought the liquor." Ms. Latimer wags her finger at me. "But unless you start making better choices, Kiara, you *are* going to end up in a place you don't want to be."

If she doesn't mean the police and juvie, she probably means the special-needs class in high school. I should have kept my mouth shut, but when people ask me stuff, I have to tell them the truth.

"But if I go to Montreal, you won't put me in special ed, right?"

Cold silence.

I press on. "I agreed to go to Montreal. So I'm going, okay?"

Ms. Latimer speaks first. "I don't know where you are going. Given all the circumstances . . . your assault of that girl—"

"She pushed my lunch tray to the floor."

Instead of telling me not to interrupt, Ms. Latimer talks right over me. As if she's not even talking to me but to Dad even though she's using *you* like she's talking to me. "Your pattern of willful, defiant behavior . . . we may have to think about a more restrictive environment for school."

Dad gets into the act. "You need more structure than I can give you. If you can't go to your mother's because of summer school, I don't know what we'll do."

My hands curl into fists. My brain sizzles and presses

against my ears. All I want to do is get out. Start over. See my mother.

Who now actually wants me.

While stomping up the stairs, I yell down, "Why don't I get something I want for once?"

Dad fires back, "Why don't you think of someone besides yourself—for once." His words sting like shotgun pellets.

A bag with a Lego castle, a Nerf gun, and a football sits on the landing. I drag it the rest of the way to my brothers' room and bang on the door.

The response is weak, muffled. "Just a minute."

Chad opens the door, wearing Max's torn and oversize pajama pants and the Boston College T-shirt I refused to wear. His face is pink and swollen, with scabs where he scraped it riding. His hair is askew, and the white crust still covers his lips. The new bandage Dad put on his arm Saturday night is dirty and curled around the edges.

I hold the bag out to him. "Here you go. Someone dropped off some toys for you. There's clothes too, since all yours got burned up."

I expect Chad to be happy that he has new toys and stuff, but he doesn't say a word. He peers into the bag for a few seconds and then lets it slide out of his hands and onto the wood floor with a dull thunk. I go downstairs to bring the clothes, hoping also to hear what Dad and Ms. Latimer have planned for me, but they've moved to the kitchen and are speaking with hushed voices.

When I deliver the bags to him, one at a time, Chad piles

them in the space between the radiator and my brothers' bunk bed without even looking inside.

"Aren't you going to open them?" I ask after I hand him the final bag, with four brand-new pairs of blue jeans. Boys' size 12. His size. I found out when I threw his ruined pants away Saturday night.

Chad shakes his head. "Don't matter."

I don't know if I'm supposed to keep saying I'm sorry for what happened to his brother and parents and his house when I already told him yesterday. He still seems sad, and I want to cheer him up because even though he's going away, he was my friend. And unlike Dad and Ms. Latimer, he isn't acting like a jerk and telling me I need "structure."

"I thanked all the people for you, so you don't have to write them a thank-you note if you don't want to."

He shoves his hands into the pajama pockets. "So what? I'm never gonna see 'em again."

"Are you going back to Iowa?"

Chad doesn't answer. Instead, he pushes past me, hitting my upper arm with his shoulder, and walks barefoot toward the bathroom. I follow him. He slams the door behind him and after a few seconds I hear him peeing. But when he's done, he doesn't come out. I don't hear him washing his hands either.

I knock on the door. "What are you doing in there?"

"Go away."

I shrug and go to my room, but I leave the door open because my room is across from the bathroom and I'll see

Chad when he comes out. I bring the article on foster homes back to my screen and rehearse the lines: *Foster parents offer loving homes to children who can no longer live with their parents and need a safe place to go.*

The bathroom door clicks open. Chad steps out. I rush out to the hall.

"Did you wash your hands?" I ask him.

"Yeah." He spits onto his hands, rubs them together, and holds them up to my face. Gross. I step backward and stumble into my door frame.

Chad wipes his spit-covered palms on my brother's pajama pants. I straighten up and step toward him. "I was looking up foster homes. Maybe if things don't work out in Iowa, you can find one near here, and we can still be friends."

"You don't know nothing," he says.

"I read about them on the Internet. They're loving homes with nice people who'll take care of you and keep you safe."

"Didn't your teacher tell you not to trust the Internet?"

I nod because Ms. Latimer once said Mr. Internet didn't have all the answers and I needed to know the source of his information. But my source this time was the state Department of Children and Families site, and the state wouldn't lie. I open my mouth to tell him, but Chad cuts me off.

"I gotta get to Brandon."

"They took him to some other state," I say. "I heard it on the news last night."

"He's all by himself."

"I know." I bet Brandon's scared. I would be if I woke up

hurting, all alone, and far from where I lived. "How are you going to get there?"

Chad clenches his fists. Heat rushes through me, and I'm sweating and shivering at the same time. In my mind, I see Chad slamming his fists against his head, his mouth wide open, screaming, *Why Brandon? He didn't do nothing to no one!* But there's nothing I can do. According to Dad and Ms. Latimer, I can't even take care of myself.

I turn away from Chad and go into my room. Outside my window is the park and beyond that the empty sky where his house used to be. I lower the shade, and my room grows dim even though it's just past noon. I run my finger along the spines of my X-Men comics, arranged in chronological order on my bookcase in the corner opposite my bed.

So many heroes. Why can't I be like them?

I pace my small room. Bookcase to door, door to bed, bed to desk, desk to bookcase. Thinking.

I left the six wrestlers on the corner of my desk, behind my computer monitor. I was going to ask Dad to send them to Brandon, but I don't know if he'll do anything for me now because he's so mad at me.

I gather the wrestlers and go out into the hall. Chad is no longer there, and the door to my brothers' room is closed. I knock.

"Go away. I don't wanna talk."

I set the plastic figures beside the door—in case Chad has special powers that I don't have and can get himself to his brother hundreds of miles away.

# CHAPTER 30

*SIX OF CHAD'S FRIENDS ARRIVE ON MONDAY AFTERNOON* after school lets out. For them, he leaves his room. They bring him a new backpack and another bag of stuff. I recognize a couple of them from school and say, *Hi, how are you?* A few mumble hello back, but the others walk off. I'm not surprised. They're the troublemakers from the regular classes who've tripped me and called me names ever since kindergarten. All of them are in the class below anyway. Two used to be in my class until one flunked fourth grade and the other flunked the year after.

My heart squeezes when they stand in our front yard talking. After a while, they go upstairs and I try to listen to what they're saying, but they don't seem to say much. Sometimes they explode into laughter loud enough to hear downstairs, but I don't hear Chad laughing. I can't imagine him ever laughing again after he tried so hard to protect Brandon and failed.

But maybe he doesn't need me to help him. He has other friends.

They leave before dinner. Chad asks to have his food brought upstairs, and Dad sends me with a plate of the spaghetti and meat sauce that I cooked. Even though Dad makes dinner most of the time now, I offered to do it tonight so he'll stop being mad at me. My brothers' bedroom, hardly larger than mine, smells sour and sweaty from the crowd of boys who were cooped up there. Two empty and crushed bags of Doritos lie in the middle of the floor. I pick them up and drop them into the trash can next to the double desk. Bags of clothes and toys remain piled up beside the radiator, and the backpack is under the bed. When I tell Chad I made the dinner, he sticks out his tongue but takes the plate anyway.

Dad and I eat in near silence. Despite my effort to help out, I think he's given up on me. I still don't know what's going to happen, if I'll have to go to summer school or get to go to Montreal, and where I'll be in the fall. So before he finishes eating the last strands of his spaghetti, I ask him.

"We're not sure yet," he answers. "We have to sign you up for summer school. But your teacher's going to see if you can retake the tests you didn't pass. If that's the case and you pass, you can leave for Montreal right away and go into regular classes in the fall." He raises his voice. "With counseling and a behavior contract."

"I'll pass them this time. I promise." But will Mami want to have me after all the trouble I've caused? And if I go, how can I help Chad get to Brandon—if Chad even needs me and if there's something a kid like me can do?

I'm just a weird girl. Not a superhero. I have no special powers. And Chad can get his own friends to help.

I scrape the hard plastic tabletop with my fingernail. "Do you think Mami will come home sooner? Like if I go and talk to her?"

Dad pushes his chair back from the table and releases a long sigh. "I hope we can work things out."

"I told her we needed her here." I pick off a piece of rice stuck to the table. "But she wouldn't listen to me." I promise myself to keep trying, as soon as I get to Montreal.

"She has to make up her own mind. And apart from the money, music means a lot to her."

I think of all the time Dad spends in the pantry. And the times he played with Mr. Elliott, which got us into this mess. "It means a lot to you too."

He nods slowly.

I go into the pantry for the banjo that now belongs to Chad. Maybe he'll want to bring it with him when he goes to see Brandon. And he'll need to take it with him when the lady from the county comes to send him to Iowa or put him in the foster home. It doesn't sound like he wants to go to a foster home any more than he wants his brother alone in the hospital. I wouldn't want to live with a bunch of strangers either, no matter how loving they're supposed to be.

My father's hand on my shoulder makes me jump. I scream.

"I'm sorry," he says, stepping back into the kitchen.

"You freaked me out." Carefully, I lift the banjo by its skinny neck.

"Where'd you get that?"

"It got blown out of their house and landed in our tree." I carry it out to Dad. "Look, not a scratch. I'm giving it to Chad, but I'm not sure he knows how to play."

Dad takes the banjo and examines it on all sides, turning it like he's roasting a pig on a spit. "His father said he started to teach him."

I put one hand on my hip. "Really?"

"That's what Big Chad said." Dad hands the instrument to me. "Take it to him. I'm sure he'll be glad to have it." My father touches my shoulder, and this time I don't flinch. "That was very thoughtful of you. Rescuing it."

"See? I don't just think of myself."

"No, you don't." He gives me a faint smile.

"Were you and Mr. Elliott friends?" I ask Dad, because he called Mr. Elliott Big Chad the way a friend would do. But a friend wouldn't have snitched to the police.

"We liked to play music together," Dad says. "But that doesn't mean we were friends."

"What's the difference?" Mr. Internet said friends are people who have interests in common with you. He told me to get involved in things other people like to do. Like riding bikes and making videos of them on their bikes.

"Friends care about each other. And help each other because they care."

I still don't get it. Enemies don't play music together. When Mami and Dad stopped playing music together,

Mami left. "So if you weren't friends, what were you?" I lean the banjo against my leg, with the heavy bottom part on my toe of my sneaker.

"Acquaintances. Acquaintances may work with each other or share one or two things in common, but that's it."

"So they don't care about each other or want to help each other?"

"Right."

I think through all the people I wanted to be my friends. Like Melanie Prince-Parker, who didn't want to be my friend. Antonio, who said he was my friend and Chad was trouble. Antonio really did seem to care about me, but now I don't know if the police are looking for him because of the party and if I'll ever see him again.

Chad.

I'm not sure I can count on Chad being my friend. Or if he can count on me being his friend because I'm not helping him get to Brandon or stay out of a foster home where he'll have to live with strangers.

"Do you feel bad for what happened to Mr. Elliott? Because you called the cops on him?"

Dad sighs. "He and Lissa put two boys in danger."

The night of the party I asked Dad what he planned to do about Chad's back. Does that make me responsible too? "Maybe I should have called." And if I'd called earlier, maybe Brandon wouldn't have gotten burned.

But maybe Chad would have been inside and gotten burned. Or maybe the house wouldn't have blown up, and no one would have gotten burned.

Dad rests his hand on my shoulder. I can tell he's think-ing too. "You should have told me sooner. But no. This wasn't something for a child to do."

I bring the banjo upstairs and knock on the bedroom door. When Chad doesn't answer, I knock louder. Then I jiggle the knob, but the door is locked. Finally, I hear a dull "who is it?"

"Kiara. I have another present for you."

"More clothes?" A pause. "Or little kids' toys?"

"No." I pluck a string and listen to the powerful twang until it dies away. "Way better than that."

The door clicks open. A bitter smell assaults me. "Where'd you get that?" Chad asks. The room is dim, lit by only one small lamp, and Chad squints in the light of the hallway. He doesn't smile.

"It was blown into one of the oak trees, so I got it down for you."

Chad twirls the banjo like Dad did. "That's my dad's."

"He can't use it now. His fingers got melted off in the fire."

Chad's face goes pale. I glance at the empty plate of spa-ghetti next to the bunk bed. Thinking about Mr. Elliott's melted fingers makes me queasy too, and I realize I said the exact wrong thing to Chad.

He seems to recover, though. "Hey, I got a surprise for you." He leans the banjo against the double desk and waves me forward.

"You're playing for me?"

"Nope." Chad flips a desk chair around for me to sit.

Then he slides the backpack from under the bed. It scrapes along the floor like something heavy is inside. He reaches in and takes out a six-pack of beer. Without the beer, the backpack lies flat. He twists one can from the plastic ring, pops the top, and hands it to me. Then he grabs another for himself.

I stare at the gold can.

His friends sneaked him beer in the backpack.

"Drink up," he says. He takes a long swallow.

I hold my breath and peer into the hole with one eye while squeezing the other shut.

"That's not what you do." He chugs the rest of his, the way I saw the kids at the party do it, and crushes the can beneath his sneaker.

"I don't want to." I set mine on my brothers' desk.

"What's wrong? You too good for it?" He leans forward, snatches the can from the desk, and pushes it toward me.

I take it, just to get him away from me. "You're not supposed to be drinking. That's why you wrecked the bike and Josh beat you up."

"I know you're not going to beat me up." He belches into my face and I shrink from the musty odor. "'Cause if you do, I won't be your friend." His tone is high-pitched, taunting me.

"I don't want to get sick like you did."

"It's not so bad. And the buzz is great," he tells me.

"Dad says you were learning the banjo." I try to change the subject, wanting to tell Chad what music means to me and how I loved hearing the chatter between his father's banjo and my father's guitar.

"Yeah?" He lifts the instrument, tunes it, and begins picking with his thumb, index, and middle finger. He plays slower than Mr. Elliott, which makes the tune sad but also melodious. After about a minute and a half, he stops and says, "That's the only song I know, 'Foggy Mountain Breakdown.' And I don't know it too good."

I don't think his father tried very hard to teach him. Even Dad played faster than that when he took his turn on the banjo.

"Did your dad learn when he was a kid?" I ask.

"Nah. He was already grown up." Chad sets the banjo on the bed behind him. "I don't remember him playing when I was little, but he went away for a while and when he came back, he was really good."

"When he went to jail, you mean?"

Chad shudders. "H-how do you know?"

"It was on TV. Three years, from 1996 to 1999."

Chad swears under his breath.

"It's okay," I tell him, ready to ask more but not sure how without making him madder.

"What? Your dad a jailbird too?" He taps the bunk bed frame. "That why your brothers way older than you?"

It does explain the gap between him and Brandon, but not between Max and me. "Nope. He had non-Hodgkin's lymphoma." Seeing Chad's puzzled expression, I add, "Cancer of the cells that make up part of the immune system. He wasn't supposed to have kids afterward on account of the treatments." I didn't intend to tell Chad all this, but now I can't stop.

Maybe it's because I'm in the room where Eli and Max first discussed why I turned out the way I did.

"The chemicals. When chemotherapy destroys the cancer cells," I explain, "it can also cause genetic mutations."

"Whatever. You sound like science class." Chad points at my can. "Go ahead, drink it. I wanna see what you look like drunk."

I stare at him, open-mouthed. Actually, I stare at his untied sneakers and behind them, the other cans of beer.

"Get it? Science class? Experiment?" He's taunting me again. I know it. "I bet you'll be reee-al funny."

I shake my head, so hard my neck cracks.

"If you drink the whole can, I'll be your friend."

His eyes bore into me like someone who knows all my secrets. I set the can on the desk again. "No." I glance up at him and back to the floor. *Friends care about each other,* I tell myself. *Anyway, he's leaving and so am I. I can't help him, and I can't be his friend.*

I stand and step toward the door. "I'm not doing any more things that are wrong just so I can have friends."

"Suit yourself. I'm not letting good beer go to waste." He scoops up the can and chugs the rest before I leave the room.

# CHAPTER 31

*NOISE FROM THE HALL WAKES ME. I TWITCH MY COMPUTER'S* mouse to kick the monitor to life. It glows in the darkness; the clock on the bottom bar reads 12:33. My wallpaper shows Chad aloft on his bike, captured in the middle of a double 360.

"You'd think after two nights ago you would have learned your lesson."

I make out Dad's voice right outside my door.

The response sounds muffled, farther away. "Leave me alone. You're not my father."

"This is my house, Chad."

"Fine. I'm outta here." I hear footsteps on the stairs, then heavier ones in the hall moving toward the stairs. "Gotta find my brother."

*Going out to find Brandon? In the middle of the night?*

"You're in no condition to—"

"So what? It's not like you care. 'Cept for your house."

I want to shout, *Don't interrupt my father!* I get out of bed and tiptoe to the door. I open it a crack and in the thin sliver of light see an empty hallway. Empty except for the stink.

Someone threw up.

Chad.

Dad raises his voice. If he hadn't already awakened me, he would have done it now. "Clean it up, Chad. Kiara and I aren't stepping around your messes."

"I don't feel good."

"Should have thought of that before you killed a six-pack."

"I only drank four. The last two are yours." Another footstep. Down the stairs.

"I don't drink."

"Well, ain't you the bomb?" A thud against the wall vibrates all the way upstairs. "My dad said he never seen a bigger wuss."

Dad steps down, toward the noise. "Get up. You don't talk that way to me."

"Really?" Chad raises his voice to match my father's. "Dad said you let Kiara talk to you like that. He said the retard walks all over you."

"Chad . . ." *Go ahead, Dad. Spank him. I'm sick of him calling me a retard.*

In the darkness I press my forehead against the solid wood of my door.

"You gonna hit me? Or put me out? Like a dog that peed on your rug?"

"Chad. Look at me. You are not a dog. Don't ever let anyone make you think you are."

Silence.

"Chad, I know that deep inside, you're a decent kid. I know that you're a brave kid. But right now, you're hurt. And you don't know what's going to happen to you."

More silence. And I wonder how Dad can be so nice after Chad said all those mean things to him.

Then I hear Chad's voice, weak and shaky. No longer tough. "I wanna go see my brother."

"You can't yet. He's too far away. But he's exactly where he needs to be to get better."

"He's scared. He's all alone."

"No one outside the hospital can see him now. Same with your parents. Too big a risk of infection." I hear another step down the stairs. Dad's solid footstep. "I'm getting you a sponge and some detergent and water."

"I'm sick, Mr. Thornton."

"I'll bring you an extra bucket."

I crawl back into bed. After a flurry of footsteps, Dad tramps to his bedroom. Chad stays on the stairs. I hear the faint sound of a wet sponge slapping against wood. Then I hear sobs, at first soft and after that . . . wrenching. I can't think of any other word to describe it. It seems to come from somewhere deep inside Chad, a sadness neither Dad nor I can understand.

I slip out of bed, change my pajamas for jeans and a T-shirt, and step into the hall. I clap my hand over my nose and mouth to filter the stench. Chad sits on the top step, head in hands. He looks up, face mottled and shiny with tears.

"You get used to the smell." His words are clear, as if he's completely sober and hasn't been crying at all. "My place stunk and we got used to it."

I stand behind him. Below us, a bucket of soapy water sits on the landing. The steps are damp and clean, but there's a puddle on the landing and splatters on the wall.

"Can you finish it, Kiara? I really am sick."

"Dad said you have to do it yourself." I take a shallow breath. "But I'll keep you company."

He grabs the banister and slowly stands, picking up a smaller bucket as he rises. Holding my breath, I step backward. He carries the bucket to the bathroom. I notice bright red streaks. Not spaghetti sauce. More like blood. He shuts the bathroom door, but I hear a dump of liquid into the toilet, a flush, and the faucet running.

When he opens the door, he grabs the frame with one hand and clutches his stomach, just under his heart, with his other. His T-shirt is crinkled in his fist, and his face is still mottled but now dry. Leaning against the wall, he slowly descends the few steps to the landing, fishes the sponge out of the bucket, and on his hands and knees scrubs the puddle from the outer edges toward its center.

"There's something wrong with me," he says, so low that I can barely hear him. "I've been sick a lot lately."

"Well, you drank too much and Josh kicked you in the stomach, and then—"

"No, it started before that." He shudders and pulls his knees to his chest. "Brandon too, but not as bad." He squeezes the sponge into the bucket. "We got beaten if we didn't clean up the house. I used to say it was my fault and not Brandon's so they wouldn't hurt him."

My mind flashes to the first time I met Brandon in the park. His grime-crusted hair that stank of fertilizer. The way he slammed the wrestlers together, one kicking the other in the face or the head. The swearwords he used when he had them fight.

But I never saw any bruises on Brandon. His skin was smooth and pale, like that of a baby. "Remember when he caught that cold and you bought him medicine?"

"It was always something with him."

Chad turns away from me, but I can tell he's crying again. I blink rapidly, trying not to cry too. Brandon had such a huge smile when we played wrestlers together. I had no idea how rotten he must have felt.

Chad loves his little brother. He wanted Brandon to have a good life.

Chad stands hunched over to wipe the wall. He hiccups audibly, his thin back jerking with each one. "I'm . . . never . . . gonna see him."

"Dad says he's at the best hospital there is. He's going to get better."

Chad leans over and spits into the bucket. "If it weren't . . . for that party . . . he'd be all right."

"Or you would have been blown up too."

"No loss." He twists the sponge against a stubborn stain on the wall.

"It was my fault. I should have paid more attention to you at the party."

"No. I wanted to . . . get wasted."

"So you'd get sick and picked on?"

"That . . . was the point." He runs his fingers along the scrubbed wall.

"What?"

Chad throws the dirty sponge into the bucket. "The biggest wipeout . . . ever. Everyone . . . watching me." He sinks to the floor of the landing, next to the bucket, and kneads his stomach. "You got the video, don't you?"

"Yeah. But if I post it, the cops are going to find it and come after us."

"So what? I'll have the most hits of everyone."

"You almost died. Do you remember?"

Chad squints at me. His hiccups seem to have stopped.

"Antonio had to give you the Heimlich maneuver," I tell him.

"I kinda don't remember. I just remember flying. Crashing into stuff. And then I couldn't breathe, but I didn't care 'cause I was flying." Chad lets his head drop to his upraised knees and mumbles into them, "But then I woke up."

I help Chad to his feet. He says lifting the full bucket makes his heart hurt, so I take it upstairs and dump it in the shower even though Dad wouldn't want me to help Chad at all.

Chad stands in the bathroom doorway. "Well, good night. And, uh, thanks."

Rogue can't touch or be touched. But most people like a hug when they're sad or sick. At her boarding school Temple Grandin built a device to give herself a hug when she was about to have a meltdown. The girls at my school would always hug the one who got hurt in PE, failed a test, or broke up with a boy. Mami used to hug my brothers and me all the time. She'd hug me during my meltdowns when I didn't want anyone touching me. While she held me, she'd sing to me in her beautiful voice, the songs from her country that would calm me down.

I miss Mami like I've never missed anyone, even Mr. Mac after he died and Mrs. Mac when she moved. And I need her to be here. Not in Montreal and me going there, the way she wants. Here—where everything happened and Dad and my friends are, where she might be able to help me help Chad. She was always the one who showed me what I had to do to be good to others, even if a lot of the time I got it wrong and made her mad.

I close my eyes and wrap my arms around Chad. "I'm giving you a hug because I think you need it," I say.

His body feels stiff at first, but then he wraps his skinny arms around my waist and lays his head on my shoulder. I realize how much shorter he is than me, and I wonder what it would be like to have a little brother, warm and hard as bone against my chest, arms, and shoulder.

Chad's tangled blond hair smells of dirt and sweat, his breath of puke, and his hands of Lysol. He's tough and mean, and sad and sick. And he's brave, so brave he would let himself get beaten up to protect someone else he loved.

I think I love Chad. I want him to have a good life. Because he's not yet ruined, and he deserves a lot better than everything he's had so far.

# CHAPTER 32

**THE SOCIAL WORKER RETURNS TUESDAY MORNING, AND** after she leaves, Dad tells me no one in Iowa wants Chad or Brandon. Their grandparents are either dead or in prison. Their aunts and uncles say they don't have room.

*This isn't Gambit,* I remind myself. Chad isn't a picture in a comic book or a plastic figure but a real live boy who needs a family to love him.

"They're looking for a foster home that can take both boys. They want Chad placed by the end of this week because he has to attend summer school," Dad says.

Which means Chad failed his classes. I'm not surprised.

"They won't treat him well," I say. "They won't love him."

Dad sighs. "He's a hard kid to love."

I stare at Dad—who didn't leave and didn't send me away when I got kicked out of school. I notice that his eyes are pale blue. "And I'm not?"

*Don't tell me what a wonderful kid I am and how lucky you are to have me because I know it's not true.*

Dad doesn't say anything. I hope he's thinking. About me. About Chad. About how no kid is perfect but we all need grown-ups to take care of us and protect us and show us how to do right rather than wrong.

I try again. "Chad wants to learn how to play the banjo. If he lives with us, you can teach him and you two can play together."

"It's a lot more complicated."

How can it be more complicated? He's already living with us. "But you're not saying he can't stay here."

Dad nods once. "I'm not saying that. Yet. But don't get your hopes up."

*How can it be more complicated?* While Dad goes out grocery shopping and makes lunch, I ask Mr. Internet. He says they prefer intact families. That means families where the father and mother don't live in different places like Willingham and Montreal. Families have to take classes in parenting and meet often with the social worker. The state has to do a background check to make sure the parents haven't committed crimes and aren't in the country illegally, which Mami wouldn't be. She has all her papers. On the good side, the state pays money to help the families and will make sure Chad gets to see a doctor and Brandon gets all the care he needs after he leaves the hospital. If Mami comes back, she won't have to clean houses. She can stay at home to make sure Chad and I don't get in trouble and Brandon gets a good start in life.

But does she want to be a mother instead of a musician?

Does she want to spend years taking care of the defective girl she wasn't supposed to have—and the two damaged boys that the girl brought home?

I return to the Google page—to the bright and happy *g*'s and *o*'s and the wide box where I can get all my question answered. But what do I ask this time?

*Getting your mother to take care of two kids no one wants?*

*Getting your mother to come home?*

I don't think Mr. Internet answers those kinds of questions. Because Mr. Internet doesn't know Mami.

Leaving the wide box blank, I push my chair back from the desk.

I have to call her. Without Dad knowing. And find some power inside me to persuade her.

Chad has a cell phone, which the cops haven't gotten around to cutting off. With a shaking hand I punch in her number. The first person to answer speaks French. Wrong number. I try again.

"*¿Eló?*"

"Mami!"

"*¿Quién habla?*"

"It's me. Kiara."

"*Dios mío.* I'm sorry. I didn't recognize the number."

"I'm calling from Chad's phone." I pause to think of how to say what I want to say next.

Bad move. Mami cuts in ahead of me. "Good thing he's leaving this week. Your father has already taken enough time off work because of this mess."

I swallow. "I don't want to go to Montreal. I want you to come home."

"Max and I have work here. And you should get away from there and all the—"

"I can't! I failed my tests . . ." I clap my free hand over my mouth. I wasn't supposed to tell her that. I'm such a bad liar.

"What did you fail?"

Now it's too late. My dream of persuading her to come home evaporates. Because I'm no good at these things. Why can't I be a superhero like Rogue and do the right thing when I need to? Why didn't I plan out what I was going to say before I got on the phone? Now I can't turn back because she'll have even more questions and I'll get in even more trouble.

My grip tightens on the phone, as if I could squeeze my mistakes out of it by pure physical force. "I failed my state tests on purpose because I wanted to stay here with my friends. But they said they'll maybe let me take them over again, and I promised I'd pass them this time. So I won't have to go to summer school. But I might be coming a little . . . late."

Nothing more about Chad and Brandon.

"I expect you to pass. Tell your father to call me tonight with the new plan." She doesn't sound as angry as I thought she'd be. "I have to go to work, but I appreciate you letting me know."

I return the phone to a frowning Chad. Even though he

stayed in his room and doesn't understand Spanish, I think he knows I failed him.

Not long after we sit down to lunch, the doorbell interrupts us. Dad goes to get it and doesn't come back for a while. "It's probably a neighbor, bringing you more new stuff," I tell Chad.

He pushes his plate toward me. He hasn't touched his grilled cheese.

Before I can ask him if his stomach still hurts, Dad appears in the archway to the kitchen. "You two have a visitor. Antonio's here with his mom."

I jump up. Chad follows. In the living room, Antonio hugs me and pats Chad's back. He tells Chad he's sorry about what happened to his parents and little brother.

"It was all over the news," he says.

Dad goes into the kitchen with Antonio's mom. Her short gray-blond hair makes me think she's a lot older than Mami.

"That party was on the news too," I whisper as soon as the grown-ups are out of sight.

Antonio shifts from foot to foot. "Yeah. The cops came to my house Sunday afternoon. Josh gave them my name."

My stomach twists. "D-do they want m-me?"

Antonio shakes his head. "Unlike that jerk, I can keep my mouth shut." He glances in Chad's direction and lowers his voice. "Just don't put any videos on YouTube of drunk twelve-year-olds wiping out, okay?"

"We coulda had a million hits," Chad mumbles.

Antonio squeezes his shoulder. "Dude, when you're the BMX champion, this'll be nothing." He pauses. "Actually . . . it'll be embarrassing."

"So . . . why aren't you in jail?" I ask Antonio, visualizing the mug shots of Veg, Brian, and Josh.

"It's not that kind of crime. Mom and I met with the lawyer yesterday, and he said I'll probably lose my driver's license for six months and get community service."

"Community service? That doesn't sound so bad." My insides relax.

Antonio smiles. "Yeah, but Veg and Dunk and I have a plan. We're going to see if we can work to maintain the bike trails over the summer. The town took them over a few weeks ago." He gives me a thumbs-up and says, "It's what's called a win-win plan."

Antonio's mother steps into the room, with Dad behind her.

"Tony, we need to go."

"Just a moment, Mom."

"Now."

He whispers, "She's my probation officer. Until I get a real one."

"I heard that." Her voice is sharp. Once again, I'm thankful my dad has been so cool about everything.

"Sorry, Mom," Antonio says, then turns to me. "I brought back your helmet, Kiara. And an extra one for you, Chad. 'Cause you're gonna use it, right?" He makes a fist and grinds his knuckle into the top of Chad's head—what the kids call a noogie.

Chad squirms backward. "Yeah, yeah, I'll use it."

"I left them on the front steps."

Antonio's mother tugs his sleeve. "Tony, I mean it. We have things to do."

Even though he's a few inches taller and muscular, he follows along like a sheep. No longer Wolverine. Not even Antonio but Tony. Before stepping through the door, he turns his head and calls out, "Bye, Kiara, also known as Rogue." He points toward me and nods. "Bye, Chad. See you around."

*Antonio called me Rogue. As if I could be a superhero . . .*

After they leave, I make a mental note to delete the party videos. I don't want anyone else to lose his freedom the way Antonio has.

But then I think about how the kids begged me to record their stunts. How they loved seeing themselves. How they talked about all the hits they got.

I think about Antonio showing me the photo of his dead father—and Mr. Elliott showing Dad the photos of Brandon.

And I think how there were no photos of Chad. Nothing to show that someone out there loves him.

Soon I will leave for the summer and he will leave for good. Unless . . .

I think about the videos again. And an idea grows.

While we clean up from lunch, I ask Chad if he'll let me interview him. I tell him I want to make a documentary about BMX freestyle riders.

I set the camera on a tripod in my brothers' bedroom. They're gone and don't need the room anymore. And because it's at the front of the house, Chad doesn't have to look out the way I do at the charred pile of toxic rubble where he used to live. If I can make it so he stays with us forever, his new room will be good for him.

We start at the beginning, Chad narrating his life story: "My name is Chad Henderson Elliott Junior. I'm twelve years old. I was born in Iowa. My entire family worked in the drug trade . . ."

I edit the interview. I make Spanish subtitles because I want Mami to understand everything. I have to look up a lot of the words in my dictionary to spell them correctly. Mami's right. I speak Spanish perfectly, but I barely know how to read and write it.

I need to find music for the sound track. A single song that will make Mami feel the same way I do about Chad.

I choose "How Long" by Jackson Browne.

I wasn't born yet when he recorded it, but it's one of the songs Mami and Dad played when they had the band, my favorite of the ones Mami sang in English. It was originally written about children killed or left to starve in the wars in Central America—children like Mami and her brothers, which is why they liked to perform it.

It's a sad song that makes me cry, but it also makes me care about a child in danger who needs people to love and protect him.

The song is a little over six minutes long. In places I fade it down and weave in the interview and my subtitles. I bring back the music when I show video of Chad soaring above the mounds on his bike—and not wiping out. I cut in the still shots: the ruins of his house, the banjo that miraculously landed unharmed in our tree, the picture of Brandon that he saved on his cell phone.

I add my voice in Spanish at the end. I never can think of the right thing to say when I'm talking to someone, but hours later it usually comes to me. So I tell Mami how much we need her, how she's helped me make my way in the world though it doesn't always look like she succeeded, and how our family has to come together to give Chad and Brandon a new home.

The last frame is black. The music has faded out. I type my name for the credits, but I need something more. A final statement.

It's three in the morning.

I stare at the screen, the letters in white, 48-point Arial, on two lines—*Producido por Kiara Thornton-Delgado.* Right before I attach the file and hit Send, I type underneath my name in 36-point italics so the words fit on one line:

*Soy super-héroe.*

I am a superhero.

## CHAPTER 33

*I HAVE FOUND MY SPECIAL POWER.*

I know this because on Thursday, the day after I send the video, Mami arrives with Max, and she has all her clothes and stuff with her. Max is driving her car back to Montreal, but Mami's staying on—except for a few weekends when she has concerts. Then she'll take the truck, and Dad will have to take time off work to watch me.

Even though Mami sometimes gets angry with Dad and me, and she's not pleased with a lot of what happened while she was gone, she's helping us because she knows what it feels like to lose everything and have to depend on the kindness of strangers.

I made her feel it with words and pictures and music.

I know I did. Because even though Mr. Internet said people with the mutation called Asperger's syndrome don't show empathy, you can't always trust Mr. Internet.

A week or so after Mami comes back, on the morning before I leave for my first day of summer school, Mrs. Mac stops by for a visit. She fans herself with a folded newspaper. Her sister's car is parked out front, and it has a scrape on the side of the bumper.

She sits on the living room sofa, and Dad sets a mug of black coffee on the end table along with a spoon for sugar. She's been in and out of town several times since the explosion, dealing with the insurance company.

Dad sits across from her and holds up the article. I read the headline over his shoulder, "Meth Couple Still Critical."

"Poor things. Over two weeks and they're still in intensive care." Mrs. Mac points to the paper with a wrinkly finger.

*Poor things?* How can she say that about them? Mrs. Elliott was so mean to her.

"At least the little boy's getting better," she says.

Dad sets the paper down and glances toward the kitchen, where Mami's studying. She's started English classes again and is also taking classes with Dad on how to become foster parents. We can't give Chad and Brandon a new home until Mami and Dad finish the state's course and pass all their tests. At least the state approved them to take the course, even though they weren't together for four months and I got into a lot of trouble then.

"The social worker told me Brandon may be released next month," Dad says. "Though he'll still have outpatient therapy and another round of skin grafts."

"We saw him two days ago," I add. Drove there and back in one long day. He was happy to get his wrestlers but began to cry and wouldn't stop when he realized Chad wasn't able to come with us. The nurse had to call a psychologist, who calmed him down and then talked to Mami and Dad while I went to the cafeteria for ice cream.

I'm finding out a lot about psychologists these days. There's one named Dr. Rose who I'm meeting with. At our first session, I called her Professor X—even though the real Professor X is a man—because she's showing me how to live in society and use my special powers for good. I already learned that we Asperger mutants really do care about other people. We just need extra help—like pictures and music—to understand other people and know what to say.

Lots of people need extra help. Chad needs it in science and pretty much all his other subjects too. Mami needs it in English and Dad in Spanish so they can talk better to each other, though Mami likes to study more than Dad does.

Mrs. Mac then asks, "Is the older boy still in the hospital?"

I nod slowly. "I think Brandon's going to get out before Chad will."

Dad mumbles his agreement while staring at his fingernails.

I remember Mami asking Dad and me—*How could you let him go on like that?*—when Chad got sick in the bathroom for the second night in a row after she got back and I told her the same thing happened several times before. Then I told her about the red streaks in the bucket. She drove him to the emergency room that night, even though I'd brought her back to give Chad a new home and Chad screamed when he had to leave.

"Chad isn't doing so good. They may have to cut open

his stomach and take some of it out," I tell Mrs. Mac. Dad gives me a look that I don't understand. But it's the truth. The doctor told Mami, and Mami told me, that Chad had inflamed patches and ulcers from his lower esophagus throughout his stomach to the top of his small intestine. Every time he ate at home, he must have swallowed those nasty chemicals along with his food. And while Brandon got burned all over his back, Chad got burned on the inside, in places people can't see but hurt just as much.

So we need to take care of him and try to give him a good life, like he's trying to give Brandon a good life.

*How do you give someone a good life?*

It won't be easy because Mami said Chad is too sad and broken to be with a family right now. After he gets out of the hospital, he's going to a place where they work with sad and broken kids the way Dr. Rose works with me, so they can live in society too. Mami seems to know a lot of stuff about these places that she won't tell me.

Mrs. Mac reaches across the coffee table and squeezes my hand. "You've been a good friend to those boys. I hope it works out so they can come live with you and you can keep on helping them."

I squeeze her hand back and force myself to look her in the eyes, like Ms. Latimer and now Dr. Rose want me to do. Hers are gray. Surrounded by enough crow's-feet for an entire murder. That's what they call a bunch of crows—a murder. "You should come back and help," I say. "There's a house for sale up our street."

Mrs. Mac laughs. "I'll certainly visit. And your mother said her mother has offered to come down from Montreal when she can. So if it works out for you and those boys, remember that you have two *abuelas* who want to lend a hand."

She pronounces the Spanish word for grandmothers "ab-you-ALE-uhs," which makes me giggle. So does the picture of Mrs. Mac's hand helping out without the rest of her.

Summer school starts with an assembly in the cafeteria, where our principal tells us to make the most of our second chance. I sit at a front table, away from most of the kids who fill the back of the room. Afterward, they all push through the door around me. I freeze, thinking of the noise, the rowdiness, the kids calling me names and tripping me.

"Out of the way, girl," says someone with a squeaky voice. Next to me is a brown-skinned boy smaller than Chad, maybe one who failed sixth grade. I shrink against the wall, hoping everyone will pass by me and leave me alone.

No luck.

"What are you doing here? You're supposed to be smart," says a tall kid with a deep voice and a Spanish accent.

Another answers, "She got kicked out. For smacking Melanie Prince-Parker in the face."

"Yeah? 'Bout time someone did it," the tall kid says.

Boys surround me. All boys. I've never seen most of them. They weren't in my classes.

But I recognize a couple of them. Chad's friends who

brought the beer. And I wish Chad were here to tutor me on how to talk to them.

"Really?" I manage, and it gives me an idea of something else to say. "You mean you don't like her either?"

"No way. Thinks she's better than everyone else." The tall kid holds out his hand for me to shake. Or slap. "I'm Mario. Wanna party with us?"

My breath catches. *Help! What am I supposed to do?*

One of Chad's friends says, "No way, Mario. Last time she partied, thirty people went to jail."

Mario takes a step back. "Are you . . . ?"

I expect him to say Crybaby Kiara. Or Crazy Kiara.

". . . the girl with the video camera?"

I nod. My throat and chest relax. My voice comes out clear. Unafraid. "Rogue two-six-six."

A little boy at the back of the circle holds up a battered skateboard. "Hey, will you make a video of me?"

"Me too!"

Now I smile. They aren't the popular girls, but they want me to make videos of them and I will—even if they're the ones that get in trouble all the time and have to go to summer school. Anyway, I got in trouble and had to go to summer school, so I'm no different from them.

"Chad showed me your videos of him," his friend says. "They're the best."

"That's because he was the best," I answer.

"You put really good music on." The kid steps aside to let another one join the group. "Chad said that's what made them so good."

My eyes sting. I want Chad to live with us so much, but I don't know if the state will pick our family or if he'll ever be well enough to live with any family.

"You seen him?" asks the kid who joined the group.

Quickly I scrape the back of my hand across my eyes. They're all watching me. But listening to me too. "Yeah. I visited him in the hospital last week. Then his brother over the weekend."

"Is Chad getting out soon?"

I shake my head. "I'm going to keep visiting till he gets out." As I talk, more ideas, more words, come to me. "Maybe we can make a video for him and I can take it to him."

"Can you make one today?" Mario asks.

The bell rings for the start of class. Quickly we set a time—half an hour after school ends. And a place—the park by the river. There aren't a lot of jumps, but the kids tell me they sometimes ride their skateboards across the street, on the steps in front of town hall.

"Sure," I say. And in my mind I make a checklist:

Bike.

Camera.

Park.

Friends.

## ACKNOWLEDGEMENTS

I would like to thank the many people who helped me to write Kiara's story and bring it to the world. I could never have done it without the support of my teachers and fellow students in the MFA program in Writing for Children & Young Adults at Vermont College of Fine Arts. I am especially grateful for the advisors who worked on the novel with me—An Na, Jane Kurtz, and Sarah Ellis—the members of my first semester workshop, and my graduating class, the Secret Gardeners.

As I worked on *Rogue*, I received the valuable advice of my critique partners and beta readers Gene Damm, Brett Hartman, Beth Janicek, Lynn Jerabek, Laura Kinney-Smith, Linda Elovitz Marshall, Mary Nicotera, Deb Picker, Lisa Rubilar, Anita Sanchez, and Beverly Slapin. The SCBWI Falling Leaves workshop gave me the opportunity to audition my early chapters, and I thank the organizers for choosing me to participate. Rachel Burk, Mario Nelson, and Judy McGlone helped me with linguistic and cultural details. Through his own work, Francisco X. Stork inspired me to write my story and then became one of Kiara's first friends.

I am fortunate to have a wonderful agent, Ellen Geiger, beside me so I never have to approach the popular girls' table alone. I thank my editor, Nancy Paulsen, and her assistant, Sara Kreger, for clearing a space at the Penguin table for me, and cover artist/ designer Marikka Tamura for making *Rogue* the best-looking book in the cafeteria.

Finally, I would like to recognize the teachers, aides, psychologists, and other school staff members working with young people with special needs to help each of us find our own special power.